The truth

"Greta, have you already met this gentleman?" M[illegible] turned to ask.

I took a deep breath and, very fast, said, "He is Herr Professor Hummel. He lives in the Brauners' old apartment. He's a piano teacher, and I'm taking lessons from him."

"What are you saying?" Mutti's voice was low, but her eyes were flashing with anger.

"Why, I think that's lovely!" Frau Vogel put in, coming up behind me. "Be reasonable, Anneliese. Greta—"

"Greta didn't ask my permission to take piano lessons!" Mutti snapped. "Why wasn't I consulted about this?"

"Because you would have said no," I wanted to say.

"Fuses the political with a strong sense of time and place. . . . [Readers] will recognize both the artist's story—how it feels to practice and practice, the nervousness, the mastery—and Greta's wish to ignore the outside world and be invisible."

—*Booklist*

"While the unusual Holocaust setting is well drawn and rings true, this is first and foremost a novel about a girl who pursues a dream and learns to believe in herself." —*SLJ*

This is **Maurine F. Dahlberg**'s first novel. She lives with her husband in Springfield, Virginia, where she plays piccolo and flute in a concert band. Like Greta, she studied piano as a child.

OTHER PUFFIN BOOKS YOU MAY ENJOY

Anne Frank: Beyond the Diary Van der Rol/Verhoeven
The Devil's Arithmetic Jane Yolen
Friedrich Hans Peter Richter
Hide and Seek Ida Vos
I Am a Star Inge Auerbacher
Missing Girls Lois Metzger

Play to the Angel

Maurine F. Dahlberg

PUFFIN BOOKS

PUFFIN BOOKS
Published by the Penguin Group
Penguin Putnam Books for Young Readers,
345 Hudson Street, New York, New York 10014, U.S.A.
Penguin Books Ltd, 80 Strand, London WC2R ORL, England
Penguin Books Australia Ltd, Ringwood, Victoria, Australia
Penguin Books Canada Ltd, 10 Alcorn Avenue, Toronto, Ontario, Canada M4V 3B2
Penguin Books (N.Z.) Ltd, 182-190 Wairau Road, Auckland 10, New Zealand

Penguin Books Ltd, Registered Offices: Harmondsworth, Middlesex, England

First published in the United States of America by Farrar Straus & Giroux, 2000
Published by Puffin Books,
a division of Penguin Putnam Books for Young Readers, 2002

1 3 5 7 9 10 8 6 4 2

Puffin Books ISBN 0-14-230145-0

Printed in the United States of America

To Randy

for helping me with the computer,

for carrying the camcorder all over Vienna,

and, most of all, for believing in me

Play to the Angel

1

Greta, stop that noise!"

My fingers sprang away from the piano as though the keys had turned red-hot.

"I'm sorry, Mutti! You were fast asleep, and I thought if I closed your bedroom door, the music wouldn't bother you."

My mother's face was white and pinched, the way it always was when she had one of her headaches. Her thick chestnut hair, usually in glossy braids wound around her head, hung in dull tangles down the back of her pink dressing gown.

She snatched up my precious book of Scarlatti sonatas. "This has your brother's name on the cover. Did you bring it down from the attic?"

I nodded. "I brought down some pieces I want to play. I don't have much music of my own."

Mutti frowned. "I hope you remembered to close the trunks afterward. You know how the attic roof leaks. I don't want Kurt's music getting wet and moldy."

"Yes, Mutti." Then you shouldn't have put it in the attic, I wanted to say. But I didn't dare—especially when Mutti was already ill.

Mutti's face relaxed a little and she patted my shoulder. "I shouldn't have snapped at you. It's just that I'd finally gotten to sleep, and then you started banging around on the piano."

Banging around! The words stung. Still, maybe if you had a headache, even *good* piano playing would sound like banging around. And I knew I'd sounded good—maybe not as good as Kurt would have, but good. In my mind, I had been playing onstage at the Musikverein, Vienna's beautiful golden concert hall. The audience had been gasping over my spirited interpretation and my delicate touch. "Such talent!" people had whispered as they applauded.

Now I was no longer a svelte, poised performer with thousands of fans but just a slightly chubby twelve-year-old with long blond braids and a secret dream.

Mutti groaned. "Look at the time! I'm supposed to go to Ilse von Prettin's for a bridge game tonight. I can't go, of course. My head is throbbing, and, besides, it's supposed to snow."

"Radio Vienna said it will snow all evening," I said happily. "It may even be our biggest snowfall of 1938!"

"I hate snow," Mutti growled.

I looked at her in astonishment. She had always loved snow. Last winter, she and I had helped Kurt build a snow goose. "Everyone makes snow*men*," he'd said. "Let's make a goose!" And we did—a glorious goose, legless and built squat on the ground, with a long neck and little button eyes. Kurt and I sat on its back while Mutti, pink-cheeked and nearly doubled over with laughter, took our snapshot.

How different she looked now, tired and ill, clutching her head with both hands as she thought.

"I'm sure Hilde can fill in for me, but our telephone is still out of order. Would you run and ask her?"

I nodded. I liked Frau Vogel. She was a lot older than my mother, and had been widowed in the Great War, long before I was born. She was Mutti's closest friend. Mutti told her all her troubles and often asked her advice. That had once seemed funny to me, because Frau Vogel could be very scatterbrained. But I'd learned that she was also quite sensible in her own way and was kind of like a mother to *my* mother.

"Then," Mutti continued, "go tell Ilse that I'm sick and that Hilde will make up the fourth. Or if she can't do it, tell Ilse to try Lilli Neff. You can stay at the von Prettins' and play with Elisabeth if you'd like."

"No, I'll come straight home." Mutti thought mean, prissy Elisabeth and I should be friends just because she and Frau von Prettin were.

"Thank you." Mutti started back to her bedroom, then turned. She looked over the piano in the same slow, calculating way I'd seen her study the cabbages in the marketplace. "Ilse was saying last week that she and Josef would like Elisabeth to take piano lessons. I wonder whether they would like to buy a piano."

Buy a piano. Buy a piano. The words echoed in my mind. I felt as if someone were sitting on my chest. I began to shake all over. From a long way off, I heard my voice say, "You—you can't mean our piano!"

Mutti's words were quiet but firm. "A baby grand piano is a big extravagance. I'm still paying off Kurt's medical bills, and sales at the dress shop have fallen off. Herr Rosenwald doesn't think he can give me a raise this year, even though he *is* promoting me to designer. Only wealthy people can afford to have dresses made these days! Besides," she continued, "the piano takes up too much room. I should have sold it last spring after Kurt died, but I couldn't bear to have people traipsing through the apartment to see it. Oh, don't frown so! We'll get a cheaper piano—maybe a nice used upright."

"But I need a *good* piano! If money's the problem, I can work several evenings a week. I can sweep floors or teach music or tutor children, whatever I have to do! Then we can keep the piano and I can take piano lessons."

Mutti was shaking her head wearily. "You have to study in the evenings. You don't want to fall behind in your schoolwork, do you?"

"But my grades are all A's and B's now, and if I'm going to be a concert pianist I need—"

"Greta, I know you enjoy playing the piano, and you are good at it. But you don't have to try to be a concert pianist just because Kurt was."

"It's not because Kurt was!" I cried.

Mutti flinched and put a hand to her head. "Do keep your voice down! You have no idea how it makes my head pound. I'm going to take another headache powder and go back to bed now. Thank you for going to Hilde's and Ilse's."

I heard her bare feet pad down the hallway to her room.

I stared at my lap, seeing my red-and-blue-plaid school jumper through a blur of tears. How could I make her understand? Playing the piano wasn't just something I enjoyed, and I didn't do it to be like Kurt. I did it because it satisfied something inside me, the way a bowl of hot soup satisfied my stomach or a breath of fresh air satisfied my lungs. But the something it satisfied was deeper than my stomach or my lungs. It was the part of me that made me *me*.

I stroked the cool, polished wood of the piano's keyboard cover. This piano was all I could count on. Kurt was gone. Mutti had gotten sharp and nervous and frail. My best friend, Erika Brauner, who'd lived downstairs from Frau Vogel, had moved to America last fall. But the piano was always there for me.

Now Mutti was going to sell it—and to the von Prettins! Of course, Elisabeth would brag about getting it. "It was Kurt Radky's piano!" she'd say, tossing her curls. But when she had to practice, she'd make faces at it. She'd play stiffly and clumsily, one eye on the grandfather clock in the corner of the von Prettins' stuffy living room.

And me? I'd have to learn to live without music. Because I knew that if we sold this piano, we'd never get another one, even a poor, cheap one. Mutti would keep saying we didn't have the money, or she'd fill up the space with furniture. Over the years, the skill would leave my fingers and the dream would leave my head. I would become merely another Viennese housewife, and the Musikverein would be just a pretty building near the city park.

Our little china clock chimed once, for five-thirty. Sick and numb, I put the book of Scarlatti sonatas into the piano bench. The Sonata in G Major, the one I'd just been playing, was still running through my head: *TAA-dada-da ta-DAA-da-da* . . . But now instead of sounding elfin and joyous, it had a plaintive, wistful air.

I put on my coat and set out for Frau Vogel's. Outside, fat flakes were spinning out of a gray sky that looked as soft as a kitten's tummy and close enough to touch. So far they had only powdered the ground, but even now I could feel that special hush that comes with steadily deepening snow. If it hadn't been for my anxiety over the piano, I would have thought it a beautiful, cozy February evening.

Frau Vogel lived on our street, Stumper Gasse. Our building was newer, but hers was prettier. Ours was slate-gray with plain windows, and hers was a pretty soft-yellow, with white plaster cherubs around the windows.

The top-floor landing smelled like a combination of sauerkraut and coffee grounds, just as it always did. Frau Vogel was a terrible housekeeper, but, like us, had to save money by doing without a maid. Still, I liked the chaos at her apartment. The radio was always playing, pots were always boiling over, and Frau Vogel was always having a crisis that I "just wouldn't believe."

"Greta! Come in, lovey!" she cried when she opened the door.

With her wide brow, bumpy nose, and short wispy hair, I'd always thought Frau Vogel looked like the bust of Beethoven in the music room at school. Tonight her big face appeared hot and flushed, and she wore a brightly flowered apron over her dress.

"You just won't believe what's happened!" she said. "I was all ready to bake a batch of my macaroons, and the oven went out. Now I'm stuck with a bowl full of dough! I thought I'd go across the hall to see whether Hannah Jacobson will let me borrow her oven."

I said, "Mutti needs you to fill in for her at Frau von Prettin's bridge party tonight. She has one of her headaches. If you can do it, I'll go tell Frau von Prettin."

"Of course I can fill in for her," Frau Vogel said, "and tell her thank you for asking. Poor thing, getting those migraines! And they're a lot worse now, since your brother passed away. I still think she should go to that Dr. Freud. Hannah Jacobson said her mother-in-law's sister had terrible back pains, and they went away after she tried Dr. Freud's talking cure. But will your mother try it? No!" She sighed. "It must be hard for you, too, having to tiptoe around and never run or laugh."

I almost added, "Or play the piano when Mutti's home." But I'd never told Frau Vogel how serious I was about my piano playing. My dream of becoming a concert pianist was like the baby bird I'd found in a nest last spring—too fragile to have even kind, well-meaning people poking at it.

"What's the latest news on the radio?" I asked, to change the subject. Frau Vogel was terribly proud of her new portable radio and kept it on all day. She even had a name for it: Eulalie. She had explained that Eulalie was a Greek name meaning "Voice of Sweetness."

She clucked her tongue mournfully. "My Eulalie is still talking about the bad news from Germany. I suppose you've heard? No? Here, come into the living room and get warm. I'll tell you about it."

She picked up an armload of newspapers from the sofa and plopped them onto the floor so we could sit down. I wondered what her bad news was. With Frau Vogel, it could be anything from a movie star's divorce to an avalanche that had killed dozens of people.

"You just won't believe it!" she said when we were settled. "You know Herr Hitler, that weasel-faced little man who rules Germany? Well, last Friday he fired his military generals. Now he commands Germany's armed forces himself!"

"I see," I murmured politely, disappointed. Some juicy gossip or a terrible disaster would have been far more interesting. To Frau Vogel, however, there was nothing as exciting as a political crisis.

"Just think!" she continued. "That madman can use the entire German military to get anything he wants." She tapped the arm of the couch meaningfully. "Including Austria!"

"Do you think he wants Austria?" I asked.

"More than anything! Some people say he won't invade us because he signed a treaty saying he wouldn't. Herr Hummel and I were talking about that just today. I said, 'Herr Hummel, you come from Germany. What do you think of Adolf Hitler?' And he said—"

"Who's Herr Hummel?"

Frau Vogel clapped her hand to her broad forehead. "I forgot you don't know him! He moved into the Brauners' old apartment downstairs when that poor woman—what was her name?—moved out."

"Frau Klodzko," I said. Tiny, ancient Frau Klodzko

had moved into the Brauners' apartment when they left for America. She had dressed in black, barely spoken to anyone, and left after only a few months—we thought to go live with her son in Poland.

"Yes, Frau Klodzko, bless her soul. Anyway, Herr Hummel's the new renter. He's a piano teacher."

"A piano teacher?" My heart thumped.

"Yes. He moved here from Munich." She lowered her voice. "He brought nothing but a suitcase! If Frau Klodzko had taken the old furniture the Brauners had left, he wouldn't even have a bed to sleep in! The first thing he did was go out and buy a big, beautiful piano. We watched the movers bring it in. The funny thing is, he doesn't have any students! He's been here two, three weeks, and never have I seen a student come. Not that I've been watching! But don't you think it's sad that he spent so much money on that big piano and doesn't have any students?"

I nodded slowly. Surely this Herr Hummel would be glad to get a student—even one who couldn't pay very much.

"And he plays so beautifully!" Frau Vogel said. "I can hear him when I go up and down the stairs. It's too bad—"

She stopped. I knew what she'd been about to say: It's too bad Kurt isn't here to meet him.

I got up and put on my coat. "I'd better go so I can let Frau von Prettin know you're coming instead of Mutti."

"Bye-bye, Greta! Tell your mother to sip some broth."

I nodded, but didn't reply. I was too excited about what I was going to do.

2

The door to the Brauners' old apartment was ajar. I knocked on it, but no one came.

"Hello!" I called softly. No one answered, so I went inside. I stood in the central hallway, from which the rooms opened out. It was the first time I'd been in there since before the Brauners had moved. It was strange to have it so silent. Erika should be standing there, grinning and saying, "I was hoping that was you!" as she bunched her long, curly gold-brown hair back into a clip. Herr Brauner's favorite American jazz records should be playing. Frau Brauner should be watering the red geraniums in the front window and turning to call, "Is that Greta? Can she stay for dinner?"

To my left, the living room door was partly open. I recognized the Brauners' shabby old brown sofa, the big pine cupboard, and the scarred little writing desk. The shaggy white rug, the lace curtains, and the brass lamp had also been theirs.

Then I opened the door wider and forgot about the Brauners. There stood the music professor's piano. It was new and beautiful, a concert grand of satiny black wood with softly gleaming keys.

I knew I should go, but the piano seemed to pull me toward it. *Bösendorfer*, the gold lettering said. Bösendorfers were made here in Vienna. They were made by hand, and many people said they were the best pianos you could buy. Kurt had hoped to own one someday.

Gently I pressed down the keys that make up a C-major chord. The depth of the sound made me step back in surprise. It was like opening your mouth and having a gorgeous operatic aria pour out when you had expected to hear your plain old everyday voice.

A music book was on the music rest. Schumann's *Scenes from Childhood*! Those were dear old friends. I had played one of them, "An Important Event," for Kurt on his seventeenth birthday as Mutti brought in his cake and presents. He had clapped, then hugged me, and even Mutti had applauded.

I looked through the *Scenes* lovingly. I had forgotten all about them, but now suddenly I couldn't wait to play them again. Surely the music professor wouldn't mind if I borrowed his piano for just a few minutes.

I sat down and began to play the first piece, "From Foreign Lands and People." Our piano was beginning to need tuning and a few repairs, but from this one the notes flowed with a silky smoothness. I could play what was in my heart, and the wonderful piano would respond.

I wanted to play the next piece and the next, but a noise outside startled me, and I jumped up. I had to go on to the von Prettins' and finish my errand.

Before leaving, I walked slowly around the living room, touching things, remembering things. The front windowsill was empty: either Frau Brauner had given away her geraniums, or they'd withered and died under Frau Klodzko's hand.

I went over to the old desk and touched its scarred drop front. Erika and I had loved that desk because it had a secret compartment under a false bottom in the center drawer. We had left each other silly notes there and had played with it until Frau Brauner said we'd break the spring. How funny to see it now, when Erika was so far away! I'd have to tell her—

Slam! I turned around. A man was standing inside the living room door, his arms folded over his gray sweater and a newspaper in one hand. He was tall and solid, with thick silver hair and a mustache. Not a choppy Hitler mustache but a fine, soft one.

"A nice desk, isn't it?" he asked coolly. His words were quick and clipped; he didn't have our soft Viennese drawl. "I plan to use it for writing letters and paying bills—unless, of course, you wish to borrow it, as you did my piano."

I felt my face turn bright red and the sweat pop out under my wool jumper. "I'm terribly sorry! It's just that—"

"What is your name?" the professor asked. He still stood in front of the door, arms folded.

"Greta Radky." I cleared my throat. "That is, Anna Margareta Radky."

"Well, Anna Margareta Radky, I am Herr Professor Wilhelm Hummel. I live here. Now, how is it that I come in from buying a newspaper and find you looking over my furniture and playing my piano as though you own not only my flat but the whole city of Vienna as well?"

"I came to talk to you, but you weren't here, so—"

"So you made yourself at home. Did you eat my dinner?"

"Why, no, of course not!"

He made a face. "Pity. I'm having liver. I hate it, but it was on sale at the butcher's. *Heh!* You didn't by any chance practice Liszt's Hungarian Rhapsody Number Ten, did you? The one in the yellow cover on the floor there?"

He was looking at me hopefully.

I shook my head, confused.

"Ah, too bad." He sighed. "Now I shall have to practice it myself. It's a terribly difficult piece. If you were going to come in here and make yourself at home, at least you could have practiced the Rhapsody Number Ten for me."

"I'm sorry, Herr Professor." I didn't know what else to say.

I thought I saw the tiniest of smiles tug at his mouth. He was pretty good-looking, I thought, even if he was kind of old. His nose was too heavy and his jaw too square to make a really handsome face. I guessed he was what adults called distinguished-looking.

"Take off your coat and sit down," he said, waving a hand toward the old sofa. "We will talk."

What a strange man, I thought, as he went to hang our coats in the entryway. I was beginning to like him, though. An awful thought came to me: What if he agreed to teach me, but turned out to be the type of teacher who just taught children to plunk through the beginner books and said "Fine! Lovely!" no matter how they played? That wouldn't help me at all.

But, I reasoned, he wouldn't have such a fine piano or be working on something as hard as the Rhapsody Number Ten if he weren't good. Besides, I had to have lessons. And any established piano teacher in Vienna would charge me far more than I could afford.

"Now!" he said briskly, sitting down on the sofa beside me. "What was it you came to talk to me about?"

I took a deep breath. "I want to take piano lessons."

"Piano lessons?" He looked startled. "Who told you I give piano lessons?"

"Frau Vogel."

"Frau Vogel! Did she make you ask me for piano lessons? Did she bribe you with candy?"

"No!" I cried, surprised. "It was *my* idea!"

His face relaxed. "I suppose it's all right, then. Frau Vogel means well, but she doesn't understand that I'm retired and don't want all the children of Vienna trooping in here to break my new piano. Now, tell me why you want to take piano lessons from me."

"I used to take lessons from my brother. He was a piano student at the Vienna Academy of Music and Performing Arts," I said proudly. "He won the Young Viennese Pianist Award two years ago. His professors said he might be the next Karl von Engelhart—you know, the retired German pianist who was so famous."

Herr Hummel's eyebrows went up. "Ahhh, von Engelhart! Of course I know of von Engelhart! Who doesn't? But why can't your brother teach you now?"

"He died last April." I hesitated. "I still practice for two or three hours after school every day, but I need a teacher. I don't know what music to work on, and I don't always know whether I'm doing things right. And now my mother . . ."

For a little while, I had forgotten that Mutti was going to sell the piano. I tried again. "She's—selling—" But the lump in my throat made my voice all high and funny, and the words ended in a sob.

The tears I'd been holding back all evening ran down in hot little streams. I wiped my face with my hand and started to get up. "I'd better go now."

"Nonsense!" Herr Hummel pushed me gently back onto the sofa. "Greta, do you like apple cake?"

"Yes, but—"

"Good!" He clapped his hands down on his knees and stood up. "I will bring us some. Frau Vogel bakes like a dream, but she seems to think I have the appetite of an elephant. She has brought me two cakes this week alone! And if I leave them on the step for the pigeons to eat, she will see. What is a man to do?"

He looked so helpless I had to smile.

"Ah, you're smiling. That's better." He pulled a big white handkerchief out of his pocket. "I have carried this handkerchief around for nearly fifty years, just in case I should meet a lovely lady who needed it! You are the very first."

He presented it to me with a bow and a flourish.

"Now dry your eyes. We will eat apple cake and drink hot chocolate, and you will tell me why talking about pianos makes you cry."

He went across the hallway into the kitchen and rattled around for a few minutes. When he came back, he was carrying a tray with the apple cake and two big cups of hot chocolate. I ate one huge slice of cake, and he cut another one for me.

"Eat the whole cake if you can," he urged. "No doubt Frau Vogel will bring me another tomorrow."

I shook my head.

"Tomorrow it will be macaroons. Her oven's broken, but she's going to borrow Frau Jacobson's if—oh!" I groaned. I'd forgotten to go tell Frau von Prettin that Frau Vogel was coming instead of Mutti. But no one would mind: the ladies knew that Mutti was often ill, and they all loved kind Frau Vogel, even if she wasn't very good at bridge.

Herr Hummel finished his own slender slice of apple cake. After he'd set his plate aside, he said, "Now, what was it you were going to tell me that called for the use of my handkerchief?"

"My mother wants to sell our piano."

"Sell your piano?" He sounded shocked.

I nodded. "She doesn't think we need it now that Kurt's gone. She says it's extravagant to keep it. The dress shop where she works isn't doing well, and we have Kurt's medical bills to pay. Kurt had hemophilia," I explained. "That means he'd start bleeding inside if he got even a tiny bump or bruise. Hemophilia runs in Mutti's family—but few women get it. Most just pass it on to their sons. One of Mutti's uncles also died of it."

Herr Hummel said gently, "Go on."

"Frau Vogel says that even when Kurt was born, he was tiny and fragile. When he was four, my parents started him on piano lessons, hoping he'd get interested in music instead of sports and games. He showed so much talent that my wealthy Great-aunt Elfriede sent my parents the money to buy him a good piano. She paid for his piano lessons, too."

"Where's your father?" Herr Hummel asked. "You haven't mentioned him."

I shrugged. "There's nothing much to mention. He left us when I was three. All I remember is that he was blond, like me, and that he and Mutti fought a lot. She says he was a dreamer—like me again, except he dreamed of making money, not music. About two years after he left, we got a letter saying he'd been killed in a train accident in Hungary."

I stopped and drank some of my hot chocolate. I

didn't know when I'd talked for so long! The piano professor really seemed to listen, though—unlike Mutti, who was always tired or ill; or the girls at school, who all had best friends who weren't me; or Frau Vogel, who meant well but had too much to say to be a good listener.

"I miss Kurt a lot, Herr Professor," I said, picturing my brother, with his brown eyes, chestnut hair, and quick grin. "He was such a special person. Lots smarter and more talented than I am. I'm sure *he* would want me to keep playing the piano. It's Mutti who doesn't understand."

I sighed. "I don't think money is the real reason Mutti wants to sell the piano. I think she just doesn't want me to play! Whenever Kurt practiced, she'd come into the living room to read or sew because she loved to hear him. But when I start to play, she says she's sick or she finds errands to run. Besides, one day after Kurt died, she put all his music in a trunk in the attic."

"She put it in the attic?"

"Yes. I was furious! She said she was trying to clean Kurt's room and there was music piled everywhere—but that was only because I'd been sorting it!"

"What did she say when she saw how angry you were?"

"We argued and she got a dreadful headache. She

gets a lot of them, but this one was so bad I finally called Frau Vogel to come."

I didn't want to say any more about that awful day. I'd been terrified that Mutti would die, even though Frau Vogel had said she'd be fine.

"I'm afraid the same thing will happen if I talk to her about keeping the piano," I finished quietly.

"I'm sorry your mother gets headaches," Herr Hummel said slowly, "but you can't give up something as important as your piano. Do you want her to sell it, knowing that you did nothing to stop her?"

"I'll try talking to her," I said. But I'd have to do it as delicately as breaking the shell of a soft-boiled egg.

"Don't try, do it! You must."

Then he asked me what music I'd worked on with Kurt. I told him, and he just nodded. I thought that was a good sign. If he'd been the type of teacher who could only teach children to plunk, he'd have acted surprised at the level of music I played.

We decided that my lessons would be after school on Tuesdays and Fridays. Herr Hummel wrote down the titles of several music books for me to bring.

Now there was just one more hurdle. "Herr Professor," I said hesitantly, "I told you we don't have very much money. Perhaps I could pay for my lessons by doing some work for you, or . . . or . . ."

Herr Hummel was raising his left eyebrow.

"You mean," he said sternly, "you have the nerve to come in here and ask me to give you piano lessons when you know that you may soon have no piano, that your mother doesn't want you to play, and that you have very little money with which to pay me?"

I felt my face burn. "Yes," I said in a tiny voice.

To my astonishment, he laughed and clapped my shoulder.

"Then, Anna Margareta Radky, I think we shall get along just fine!"

3

The next day, Wednesday, the sun was warm enough to melt most of the snow—but only a few of its rays could squeeze through the tiny windows of the storage attic. I wrapped my sweater more tightly around me as I sat on the cold floor late that afternoon, surrounded by piles of piano music.

I had already found the étude books Herr Hummel had asked me to bring to my first lesson, and had taken them downstairs. Now I was sorting the rest into alphabetical order. I'd made a game of seeing which pile would be the highest. The "C" pile, with its Clementi, Chopin, and Czerny, had a good chance, but the "B" pile, with Bach, Beethoven, and Brahms, was close behind. And now that I was finding more Scarlatti, adding it to the music of Schumann, Schubert, and Scriabin, the "S" pile was doing quite well.

I stood up, wiggled my stiff shoulders, stretched my legs. It was time to walk around and get the numb pins-and-needles feeling out of my feet.

My family's section of the attic was stuffed. Steamer trunks held old clothes and lengths of fabric Mutti had intended to use someday. A black suitcase was tagged "Greta's toys"; a green one, "Kurt's schoolbooks." Mutti's old skis stood in a little alcove. Across from them, in the shadows, stood Kurt's braces.

I ran my fingers over them. Ugly iron contraptions they were, things you'd wear in hell. And Kurt had been in hell whenever he'd had one of his bleeding episodes: a bruise or bump could cause him to bleed into a knee or an elbow. The joint would become huge and hard, like a grapefruit, and deep purple. After a while—a long, agonizing while—it would lock into a bent position, and he would have to wear one of these braces to straighten it out.

When I was eight, I had wanted to try on one of them. I'd just slipped my foot into it when Mutti found me. "That's not a toy!" she'd snapped and swatted my leg, hard. I'd cried, not because of the swat, but because I'd never *thought* it was a toy. I'd just wanted to see what it was like, to know how Kurt felt when he had to wear it.

"Greta, are you in the attic?"

"Yes, Mutti!" I scurried away from the braces, as though I was afraid that even now she'd be angry if she caught me touching them.

I put the piles of music in the trunk, closed it, locked the door to our section, and ran to meet Mutti in the stairwell.

"I hope you haven't been up here long," she said, giving an exaggerated shiver. "It's freezing."

"No, not very long." I knew I should tell her, boldly and briskly, that I'd been sorting music, that I needed to put it in order because I was starting piano lessons tomorrow.

But I didn't. I couldn't seem to be bold and brisk with Mutti, only timid and hopeful. Herr Hummel didn't understand. But he hadn't seen Mutti ill, the way I had.

"How was work today?" I asked.

"Not bad." Mutti unlocked the door to our apartment. "We got several more dress orders at the shop, and Herr Rosenwald thinks that things are looking up. *And* he said that Frau Waldmann and Frau Wilhelm asked for me personally, to design their gowns!"

I gave her a kiss on the cheek. "They should! You're the best seamstress and dress designer in Vienna."

"Thank you." Mutti returned my kiss. "I thought we could go to Café Adler to celebrate."

"Why don't we go to Schöner's instead?" I suggested. "It's no farther than the Adler, and the food's so much better."

Mutti collapsed in the green chair beside the coal

stove and put her feet up on the footstool. "No, I don't like Schöner's. The food is too rich, and the prices are too high. Besides, it's noisy. I want to go to a quiet place like the Adler."

I should have known she'd say that. When Kurt was alive, we'd go to gay, fashionable places like Schöner's or the restaurant at the Hotel Sacher—or if the weather was fine, maybe we'd get an outdoor table at the Kursalon in the City Park. At those places, you got thin schnitzels, fresh dumplings, and light-as-air pastries, served on elegant china plates. Music played, people laughed, and carts with fantastic desserts rolled by. There was plenty of what we Viennese called *Gemütlichkeit*—the joy of being alive, of being in Vienna!

At the Adler, the atmosphere was as dull as the food. Frau Vogel and Mutti's other friends kept saying, "Anneliese, that's the only dreary eating place in all of Vienna! Why do you go there?" Mutti would shrug and murmur, "I don't know. It just suits me somehow."

"All right," I said, "we'll go to the Adler." Then, after Mutti had rested and eaten, I would talk to her about keeping the piano.

But everything seemed to conspire to put Mutti in a bad mood.

First there was the weather. Much of last night's snow had melted off during the day, but the remaining slush and wet spots were quickly freezing into ice. We held on to each other as we picked and slid our way around the icy patches.

"Won't winter ever be over?" Mutti said, groaning, after a slick spot had nearly thrown us both on our backsides.

Then we saw a little street musician at the corner where Mariahilfer Strasse met Amerling Strasse, the street where the von Prettins lived. The musician wore a dirty, too-large coat and held a concertina. When he saw us coming, he smiled and began to play a happy little polka. He played well, and I felt sorry for him, having to be outside. Vienna had a lot of beggars and street musicians, and I hated to see them shivering in the cold.

I felt around in my coat pockets, but all my money was in my little china savings-bank at home. "Mutti," I whispered.

She tossed a couple of coins into his cup. Not much, but he bowed and said, "Thank you, lovely lady."

Mutti just turned up her nose and walked on. I looked back and smiled at the little man, but she pulled me away.

"I'm tired of seeing beggars everywhere," she said peevishly. "In Germany, the government finds jobs for them. Why can't our government do the same?"

I was surprised and hurt. Kurt had always talked with the street musicians we saw. A lot of them had had steady jobs playing at cafés or in theaters before times got so hard for people in Vienna. They were proud that they still had a way to earn money—even a few Schillings in a cup—and didn't have to beg. Usually Mutti gave them money and wished them well. But tonight she seemed to be looking for reasons to be annoyed.

Then there was the tough cabbage. Few Viennese thought the Adler's food was worth coming out for on such a cold evening, so we got our orders quickly—flat, heavy goulash soup for me and stuffed cabbage for Mutti. She soon tossed down her knife and muttered that she'd cut taffeta that was more tender than her cabbage leaves.

"You can have some of my goulash if you like," I offered, proud of myself for not saying that we should have gone to Schöner's.

"No, thank you." She pulled open one of the cabbage leaves and ate the filling. "How was school today?"

I told her about how Hedi Witt, who sat by the

window in German grammar class, had eaten a handful of snow off the outside window ledge and then made awful faces because she'd swallowed a bug, and Frau Hoffmeyer never figured out why we were all laughing.

Mutti chuckled. She remembered strict, half-deaf Frau Hoffmeyer from when Kurt was in her class.

Now's a good time, I thought. "Mutti, we must talk about the piano." That sounded good. Bold and brisk. "I know we could use more money, but I don't think you understand how much the piano means to me."

"I told you we'll get another piano," Mutti said wearily. "Besides, I won't sell it to the von Prettins unless they agree to pay what I want. I know they have the money, and I won't put up with any tricks from them, even though Ilse *is* my friend."

"But even if they *do* agree to your price, you still can't sell it! The piano's my life, my—"

Mutti put her hands up to her temples. "Please don't raise your voice like that! I can't talk about this when I'm tired. Now, are you ready to go?"

It's never a good time to talk about it, I thought angrily. But maybe the von Prettins wouldn't offer enough money and we'd get to keep the piano, after all. Frau Vogel always said that Herr von Prettin prided himself on being cunning with his money. Perhaps things would work out on their own.

Please, God, I thought, let Herr von Prettin be so wily that he annoys Mutti!

• • •

Friday afternoon at school dragged. How could I concentrate on the Battle of Vienna or English verbs when my first piano lesson was in only a few hours? I tuned out my teachers' droning and thought: What will Herr Hummel have me play? Will he think I am good? What kind of teacher will he be?

"Greta Radky!"

Frau Werner, our history teacher, was looking straight at me. "Do you know the answer, Greta?"

The classroom was silent. Elisabeth giggled.

Next to me, plump Käthe Neff put a hand in front of her mouth and whispered, "Question fourteen!"

I looked down at my history book. Question fourteen was "Who led the Viennese against the Turks in 1529?"

"Count Salm," I said, remembering my homework lesson.

"Thank you." Frau Werner nodded. "Please pay more attention in the future. Now, Elisabeth, since you think history is so funny, you may answer the next question."

Finally the clock hand slid to the half-past mark, the bell rang, and we were free. With the other girls, I curtsied to Frau Werner. I wanted to thank Käthe, but she had walked on ahead with Hedi Witt, who was her best friend. Hedi's short auburn curls hung close to Käthe's dark brown bob as they talked.

I sighed. All the girls in my class were paired off, including Erika's and my old friends: Käthe and Hedi, Paula Kovacs and Annemarie Klenk. Once it had been Greta and Erika, but now it was just me. The only other girl in our class without a best friend was Elisabeth, and I didn't want to be paired off with *her*.

I stopped at our apartment to drop off my books and get my music, then went to Herr Hummel's. I knocked on the door several times, wondering whether he had forgotten my lesson.

Finally I heard footsteps inside.

"Ah, come in!" Herr Hummel cried when he opened the door. He was wearing a worn, nubby sweater, the exact blue of his eyes. "Forgive me for taking so long. I'm afraid I dozed off."

"I'm sorry I woke you."

"No, it's very good that you did!" he replied, taking my coat and hanging it on a hook in the entryway. He shook his head, looking puzzled. "I was having a bad dream. There was a young man chasing me through

Vienna, a piano student I knew back in Munich. I hadn't thought of him for months! I suppose it was listening to all the news about the Nazis that made me dream of him."

"Was he a Nazi?"

"Oh, the best sort of Nazi! Arrogant, obnoxious, a bully."

I hoped he'd say more about his life in Munich. To my disappointment, he waved a hand and said, "But that horrid boy is in the past now and that's where he'll stay. Now, tell me, have you talked to your mother about keeping the piano?"

"I tried, but she was tired and wouldn't listen. I'll try again, I promise."

He looked disappointed. "All right," he said. "I shall trust you to do it. Here, warm your hands at the stove a bit before you begin playing."

He had me start with the book of piano études that I'd worked on with Kurt. And I quickly found out one thing: he was no teacher for plunking children.

After I had played a couple of easy études, he flipped to the back of the book, where things got difficult. The key signature was five flats, and little black notes zigzagged up and down the page.

While I played, Herr Hummel paced the floor beside me and gesticulated and gave directions in a voice that was soft but intense—almost excited. "Smooth out the trill. That's better. Now linger a bit on the first note of each measure. Louder. Softer. Softer still. Play the accents more gracefully, not *whomp, whomp*! Make your staccato notes less like thorns and more like tiny sharp snowflakes—the ones you barely feel before they melt on your face. Remember the double flat in the left hand."

And I had to do all this while my fingers raced over the keyboard playing music I'd never seen before.

We did two more études, me playing and him pacing. When I'd finished the second, which was the last one in the book, he stared at me for a moment, his blue eyes piercing me and his fingers drumming the top of the piano. Then he asked questions: How long had I played piano? Who had I said my brother was? Had I performed anywhere yet? Why not?

"There's been no place for me to play," I said simply. "Kurt used to say that maybe he and I could do a recital together someday. I—I used to dream of it. But he was always busy with his own auditions and competitions, and then he got sick the final time and . . ." I shrugged. "Then it was too late."

More drumming of fingers and piercing with eyes. I wanted to ask *him* some questions: Do you think I'm good? Why do you want to know whether I've performed yet? Why are you staring at me like that?

Finally he said, "I want some people to hear you. Let me see what I can do."

Before I could ask any questions, he went over to the cupboard, pulled out a book, and brought it over to the piano. He looked through the book, thinking.

"I want you to play some real music now. Have you played the Mendelssohn *Songs Without Words*?"

I shook my head.

He put the book in front of me. Opus 19, it said, Number 6.

"I'll keep quiet," he said, sitting down in the little chair behind me. "I want to hear what you make of this on your own. It's slow and not at all like the études."

I began nervously. It had been easier to play when he had paced and given directions. Then we had both been involved in making the music. Now only I was making the music, and he was listening intently.

After I'd finished the piece, he said, "That was nice, but you must play more boldly! Don't be timid. Try to sound the way you did when I came in from buying my newspaper. You weren't holding back then."

I started again, trying to let the notes sing out as I did when I was having my Musikverein fantasies.

"More still!" Herr Hummel cried. He jumped out of his chair and swept one arm through the air. "Make your sound fill all of Vienna, all of Austria!"

He motioned for me to follow him. "Come, let me show you something."

He went over to the window, the one that looked out on Stumper Gasse. In front of the white lace curtains a tiny blue-gowned angel doll was suspended from the ceiling by two nearly invisible threads, so that she looked as if she was flying.

"She's beautiful," I told Herr Hummel, wondering what she had to do with my playing.

He smiled proudly. "She is one of the few things I brought from Germany. She loves piano music, so I put her where I can play to her. And you must play to her, too. Let your sound project and your feelings come through to my little angel. Can you do that?"

I nodded. This time when I played, I thought of the angel wanting to catch every nuance of Mendelssohn's Song. I heard Herr Hummel say, "Good." So I relaxed, and soon I got so involved in the sweet, sad music I forgot to be shy.

"Fine!" Herr Hummel cried when I'd finished. "You mustn't ever play timidly. It's better to play something wrong."

He had me play another Mendelssohn Song, a Scarlatti sonata, and a short Schumann piece. He corrected me a few times, but he said that for today he mostly wanted to hear how I did them on my own. I could work on technical details later.

After I'd played the Schumann, I was surprised at how tired I was. I was glad when Herr Hummel said, "Enough work for today. Let's have some hot chocolate and finish off the apple cake."

While he was in the kitchen, I took a closer look at the little angel. Like many angel dolls, she was wearing a blue satin gown and had flowing brown hair and feathery wings. But, unlike the faces of others I'd seen, hers wasn't simpering. She had a wise, understanding look. Her clear, calm eyes seemed to gaze directly at me. Her mouth curved up a little, as if she saw a touch of humor in life. She looked like the kind of angel I wanted watching over me: intelligent, caring, ready to listen.

Herr Hummel set the tray on the coffee table. "Ah, you're admiring my little angel! She was made in Paris in the last century. My father gave her to my mother the first Christmas they were married, to put at the top of their Christmas tree. I couldn't bear to leave her behind in Germany."

"Herr Professor," I asked carefully, "did you leave because you were—well, in trouble?"

He thought a moment, then said slowly, "In Nazi

Germany, if you are a decent person, you are *always* in trouble—either with the government or with your own conscience. That is why I left."

I opened my mouth to ask him more, but he said, "No, it's my turn to ask you something. Frau Vogel told me that your best friend used to live in this flat. She wasn't the old woman in black who was getting into a cab when I first arrived, was she?"

I giggled. "No, that was Frau Klodzko! She just lived here for a few months. Before her was when my friend Erika Brauner lived here. Her father got transferred to New York last fall."

"You must miss her."

I nodded. "We met when we were five. Mutti was visiting Frau Vogel and sent me out to the courtyard to play. Erika's parents had taken her to see the white Lipizzaner stallions. She told me about them, and we pranced around for hours, playing horse! After that, we were always playing something: empresses, brides, American cowgirls. Then when we outgrew make-believe, we rode bicycles and talked—mostly talked."

"Do you write to each other?"

"Yes. But she has a new friend, Rosemary." I scowled. "They do everything together, the way she and I used to."

"Ah, I see," Herr Hummel said, patting my shoulder

sympathetically. "Sometimes it's easier to be the one who leaves than the one who is left behind."

I smiled at him.

On the way home, I wanted to dance and squeal and toss my music books in the air. Herr Hummel thought I was good! He believed in me and wanted to keep teaching me! And I could tell that he was a good teacher—a serious, experienced professor who could teach me the kinds of things I needed to learn. Everything had worked out perfectly!

Well, not perfectly, I remembered. Not yet. Not until Mutti said we could keep the piano. Herr Hummel couldn't teach me—no one could teach me—if I didn't have a piano to practice on.

4

I had hoped that Saturday afternoon I could hurry home from school and practice, then finish sorting the music in the attic. But my teachers had other plans for me.

"Don't they think we have anything to do but study?" I grumbled to myself as I turned onto Stumper Gasse. Before Monday morning, I had to prepare for a test on fractions *and* one on German grammar, and translate three pages of Latin. I also had to start writing an essay—in English yet!—on "The Best Day of My Life." The idea of doing it in English didn't bother me. I'd helped Erika practice her English last summer, when she and her parents had taken private lessons. But I didn't know what to write about.

I had asked Frau Schäffer, our English teacher, whether we could write about what we thought the best day of our life *would* be. She had said no, of course not, because the whole point was to practice our past-tense verbs. That meant I couldn't do mine on the day I would be a guest soloist with the Vienna Philharmonic. Now I didn't know *what* I'd write about. There had been some beautiful days before Kurt died, but I didn't want to write about them. Someday maybe I'd be able to—but not now, not yet.

I unlocked the door to our building. How nice it would be to get to our apartment, drop my coat and heavy book bag in a chair, and start practicing. Unless Mutti had come home early, as she sometimes did on Saturdays. Then I'd go on up to the attic and—

I stopped halfway up the stairs.

I could hear piano music! Mozart. *TAA-da-da, ta-da-da-da-DAA-da-da.* Played badly.

Who in our building besides us had a piano?

Nobody.

I ran up the stairs, stuck the key in our door, and pushed it open.

"That was lovely, Ilse!" Mutti was exclaiming.

"I haven't played for years." Frau von Prettin laughed. "But I love that piece. Mozart, isn't it? Or—oh, Bach or someone! I've always thought it sounded like butterflies flitting among the flowers."

More like elephants doing gymnastics, the way she was playing it. I scowled at the von Prettins behind their backs. Frau von Prettin was an older version of

Elisabeth: dainty, with blue eyes and blond curls, although her hair was swept up on top of her head, whereas Elisabeth's hung down her back. Herr von Prettin was tall and craggy. He had always reminded me of an eagle, with his penetrating eyes and long, bony nose.

I tried to sneak past the living room door, but Mutti turned and saw me.

"Ah, here's Greta!" she said. "Come say hello to Elisabeth's parents!"

"*Küss die Hand,*" I muttered to them as I went into the living room. Kiss their hands, indeed! But that was what polite Viennese children had to say to adults.

"Your mother was just telling us what a fine piano this is," Herr von Prettin said, fixing me with his eagle eyes. "You play, don't you? Do you think it's a good piano?"

"It—it needs tuning and some repair," I stammered.

They all laughed, as though I'd said something cute.

Herr von Prettin said haughtily, "I'm sure your mother will take that into consideration when we settle on the price."

"Certainly," Mutti quickly agreed.

I should have known that Mutti would agree to anything Herr von Prettin wanted. I couldn't totally blame her. He had a commanding air, as though he was used to people obeying him, and expected them to. Erika had told me once that even our teachers were afraid of him.

"I have a splendid idea!" Frau von Prettin cried, clapping her hands. "Greta, you play something for us!"

"I have to start my homework," I said stiffly.

As I went down the hallway to my room, I heard Frau von Prettin say, "Ah, the poor dear, she's too shy."

Herr von Prettin said, "If Austria comes to its senses and lets Adolf Hitler take over, Greta and Elisabeth can join a *Jungmädel* group for young Nazi girls. *Jungmädel* get to be in parades and go on campouts. It's good, wholesome fun."

"It sounds like just what Greta needs," Mutti said.

"Elisabeth's cousin Dagmar loves it," Frau von Prettin put in. "When Herr Hitler went to Stuttgart, she even got to march in the parade to welcome him!"

I couldn't think of anything more horrid than marching around with Elisabeth von Prettin, singing about unfurling flags and undying loyalty. She made the perfect daughter for Herr von Prettin, I thought: the kind who would curtsy prettily and say, "Whatever you wish, Vater," and bring home good grades, and charm him into spoiling her. Of course, he wouldn't see the Elisabeth *I* saw: the one whose eyes slid over to Annemarie Klenk's math tests so she could copy the answers, the one who'd blamed Käthe Neff for upsetting Frau Szabó's ink bottle in Latin class when we all knew she'd done it herself.

I tossed my book bag and coat on the bed and sat down at my desk. I couldn't study, though. I listened to the von Prettins and Mutti talking.

"I'll have to think about the price," Herr von Prettin said. "It's higher than I want to pay, but it's much cheaper than a new piano. If we do decide to buy it, we'll need it on March eighth. That's Elisabeth's birthday. We want to move it in while she's at school."

"She'll be so surprised!" Frau von Prettin exclaimed. "We'll let you know what we decide, Anneliese. And tell Greta not to say anything about it to Elisabeth!"

After they left, Mutti came into my room. I pretended to be studying.

"They're going to think about it," she said.

I didn't look up from my math book.

"Oh, Greta, don't make this harder than it has to be!" she burst out. "I told you, we need the money. If the von Prettins will buy the piano for what I want, I'll have to sell it to them."

I didn't answer.

She gave a long sigh. "I have to run to the market before it closes. Don't forget that we're going to Frau Vogel's at four for coffee. Wear your green wool dress."

After she left, I went into the living room to practice. There was a dirty ashtray on the piano! Wrinkling my nose, I took it into the kitchen and emptied it. But the piano, the living room, the whole apartment still smelled of Herr von Prettin's cigarettes and his wife's too-sweet perfume.

What if the von Prettins agreed to Mutti's price? "It's much cheaper than a new piano," Herr von Prettin had said. How could I bear to watch the movers pack my piano in a crate and take it away? Or to see the emptiness where it once had been?

Angrily, I opened my book of études and banged out the first exercise Herr Hummel had assigned me. Tears filled my eyes and dropped onto the piano keys. Soon I couldn't see to play anymore.

I put on my old green wool dress and brushed my hair. I didn't want to go with Mutti to Frau Vogel's and have to smile and eat pastries, but I didn't want to stay here either. Not with the lingering smell and sound of the von Prettins.

Mutti got home and changed quickly into her good peach-colored knit dress. We put on our coats and boots and set off down Stumper Gasse. I wondered what Mutti would say if Herr Hummel was playing his piano when we went past his door. Or what if we met him on the stairs and he said hello to me?

But my teacher's apartment was silent, and we ran into no one as we clomped up the stairs in our winter boots.

"Ah, Anneliese and Greta!" Frau Vogel hugged us as though she hadn't seen us for years. Then she rolled her eyes. "You'll never believe what's happened! The stove has been fixed, but I found bugs in the flour! *Bugs*, can you imagine? Tiny black ones. I've never been so upset! I ran down to Hermann's Confectionery for our pastries—and of course I still have plenty of macaroons—but I had *so* counted on making a lovely torte for us!"

"I'm sure everything will be fine, Hilde," Mutti said, and the two of them exchanged kisses on both cheeks.

"I hope so." Frau Vogel sighed. "Now, give me your coats and go along into the living room. There's someone I want you to meet."

I started to follow Mutti into Frau Vogel's warm, cluttered living room, but stopped short in the doorway. There on the sofa sat my piano teacher.

"Herr Hummel!" I gasped.

"Good afternoon," he said. He stood and bowed courteously.

"Greta, have you already met this gentleman?" Mutti turned to ask.

I took a deep breath and, very fast, said, "He is Herr Professor Hummel. He lives in the Brauners' old apartment. He's a piano teacher, and I'm taking lessons from him."

"What are you saying?" Mutti's voice was low, but her eyes were flashing with anger.

"Why, I think that's lovely!" Frau Vogel put in, coming up behind me. "Be reasonable, Anneliese. Greta—"

"Greta didn't ask my permission to take piano lessons!" Mutti snapped. "Why wasn't I consulted about this?"

"Because you would have said no," I wanted to say. But Herr Hummel was walking over to us. He gave Mutti a smile that would have melted the ice outside.

"Frau Radky," he said quietly, "I am Herr Professor Wilhelm Hummel. I have the pleasure of giving your daughter piano lessons."

"Why—but—" Mutti stammered. She looked confused, as if she didn't want to be friends with my piano teacher but could hardly be rude in return for his courtliness.

"You must be cold after your walk," Herr Hummel said. "Why don't you sit in the chair beside the coal stove? Here, let me escort you."

He gave her his arm, and Mutti walked with him into the living room.

From behind me in the entryway, Frau Vogel chuckled. "That man's a charmer, isn't he?" she whispered. "Let's hope he can win over your mother!"

I turned to smile at her, and we joined Mutti and my teacher in the living room.

Herr Hummel was saying to Mutti, "Frau Vogel has told me that you are a dressmaker at Herr Rosenwald's shop. I am quite impressed! People say that Herr Rosenwald's shop makes the finest gowns in all Vienna."

"Thank you." Mutti's stiff smile seemed to soften a bit.

There was silence for a few moments. Then my professor tried again. "With a name like Radky, your husband must have been Czech."

"Yes. My husband grew up here, but his family was from Prague. One of his aunts and some cousins still live there."

"You must visit them!" Herr Hummel cried. "Prague is a beautiful city. I have played there, at the National Theater."

"You've played at the National Theater?" I asked in astonishment. "Why, the best musicians in Europe perform there!"

"Yes, I've played there," he murmured. Then, quickly, before I could ask anything else, he said, "Frau Radky, let me tell you where to get the best meal in all of Prague. There's a little stand right next to the railway station. The old man who runs it will sell you a *parek* the thickness of my wrist—not the tiny little excuses for sausages that you get at most stands!"

"But when did you play at the National Theater?" I persisted.

"It was long ago," he answered quietly but firmly. "Now, Frau Vogel, are we ready for our afternoon coffee and cake—our *Jause*, as you Viennese call it?"

"Greta and I will bring in the trays," Frau Vogel said.

Frau Vogel whipped cream for the coffee while I arranged the food on her best silver tray. We had rolls and butter, Alpine cheese, the macaroons, and two kinds of pastry: apricot and plum.

I asked her, "Has Herr Hummel talked to you about the places he's played?"

Frau Vogel shook her head. "He's very modest. Every once in a while he forgets himself and mentions the times he's played in Prague or Paris or Berlin, but he doesn't seem to want to talk about his life. I try not to ask him." She leaned toward me and added in a whisper, "He may have a Past!"

With Frau Vogel, a Past meant a scandalous love affair. I couldn't see Herr Hummel as having had one of *those*, but I guessed I shouldn't ask him any more questions. You never knew.

When we got back to the living room, Herr Hummel cried, "Frau Vogel, how wonderful! You've truly outdone yourself!"

"It's mostly from Hermann's, I'm afraid," Frau Vogel replied.

"But you, clever lady, knew what to order and how to arrange it," he insisted. "If I had been in charge, we'd no doubt be having some dreadful concoction. Fried horsemeat rolls, perhaps, or boiled puppy-dog tails, served on tin plates."

Even Mutti had to laugh at that.

"Oh, go on with you!" Frau Vogel chuckled and blushed with pleasure. "Anyone who plays the piano the way you do must have exquisite taste in all areas of life! Anneliese, you should hear him play! Never have I heard such music! He's even better than K— I mean—"

She stopped. Now her face was as red as the flowers on her dress.

"I'm sure he's quite good," Mutti murmured stiffly.

Then she snapped, "Greta, leave some cream for the rest of us!"

We ate silently, feeling awkward. Eulalie was softly playing Johann Strauss's *Voices of Spring*, but the gay melody seemed to hit our ears and bounce off without doing its job of making us happy.

Finally Herr Hummel put down his fork and said, "Frau Radky, perhaps we should talk now about your daughter's piano lessons."

Mutti started to open her mouth, but Herr Hummel continued.

"I have asked Greta to come twice a week for lessons. I know that you suffer from headaches, but Greta says she is careful never to bother you with her practicing. I hope you won't mind if she continues to practice while you are out and cannot hear."

He gave her another one of his disarming smiles. Mutti blinked at him. Then, as though it were a speech she'd memorized, she said, "I've already offered to sell our piano to friends. We need the money. Besides, our apartment is very small. It's ridiculous to have that piano when we must eat off a tiny kitchen table."

Herr Hummel leaned forward intently and rested his forearms on his knees. "I don't think you understand. Greta is an excellent pianist. Her brother taught her well, but she needs to begin lessons again now. And it's *not* ridiculous for her to have a piano. It's necessary—much more so than having a dining table."

Mutti shook her head firmly. "We can't afford piano lessons, Herr Professor! Greta never should have told you we could. Kurt's great-aunt paid for his, but we can't ask her to pay for Greta's as well."

"Greta is paying for her lessons by working for me," he said.

I blinked at him. "I am?"

"Why, yes." He smiled. "You're working very hard by practicing every day. And you, Frau Radky, can also help pay for the lessons by keeping your piano. That's all the payment I want."

"That's very kind, but we still need to sell the piano to get money for other things." Mutti sounded as if she was trying hard to be patient. "For Kurt's medical bills and—and just for us to live on! Herr Rosenwald's shop isn't doing as well as it used to, and—"

"You said it's doing better now," I ventured timidly. "Remember? You said you had some new orders and that Herr Rosenwald thought things were looking up."

Mutti said reluctantly, "We're doing a bit better, I suppose. But things aren't the way they used to be!"

Frau Vogel banged her coffee cup down on its

saucer. "I say for shame, Anneliese! Wanting to sell that piano, when you know that Greta enjoys playing it! If you need the money so badly, why don't you sell that antique cupboard in Kurt's old room? Nobody is using it, and you know how Helga Müller downstairs admires it! She has told me she'd give you quite a sum for it."

"Not as much as I can get for the piano," Mutti argued.

I had an inspiration. "But don't forget that you promised to buy me a new piano. If you subtract that from the money you'll get for our *old* piano, the cost might come out the same as if you kept the old piano and sold the cupboard."

Mutti's lips were pressed tightly together, as though they were all that held back a torrent of angry words. I turned my eyes downward to my lap, but not before I saw Herr Hummel smile and wink at me.

"Greta is right!" Frau Vogel said happily.

"But I promised the von Prettins they could buy our piano," Mutti insisted. "I can't just tell them I've changed my mind."

Eulalie was murmuring, "Official announcement . . . Adolf Hitler . . . this morning . . . talks taking place . . ." I was glad the adults didn't hear. I wanted them to keep talking about the piano.

"Perhaps I have a solution," Herr Hummel said thoughtfully. "The Jacobsons across the hall are trying to sell their piano. They asked me to try it. It's a good piano, and they are willing to sell it for a low price so they can leave Austria. They know how much Adolf Hitler hates the Jews, and they want to leave for fear he and his Nazi Party will take over here. I can tell them to offer their piano to the von Prettins. It may not be as fine a piano as yours, but it's tuned and in good condition."

"But—"

"But nothing, Frau Radky," Herr Hummel said flatly. "You must think about your daughter."

"I've told her we'll get her another piano—someday, when we have the money."

"Someday will be too late!" Herr Hummel said firmly. "Musicians must stay in practice. Besides, I am hoping that Greta will agree to play in a recital next month."

I gasped. "A recital! Next month? Where?"

"At the Academy of Music and Performing Arts."

Me? In a recital at the Academy?

Mutti was staring at Herr Hummel. "Are you just saying that so I'll keep the piano?"

My professor shook his head. "Herr Doctor Lothar Haas, who teaches piano at the Academy, is a friend of mine. He sponsors a recital every year for talented young pianists such as Greta. I told him yesterday that I would like for her to perform this year, if she agrees to do it."

I had a chance to play at the Academy. That was what Herr Hummel had meant when he said, "I want some people to hear you. Let me see what I can do." I'd thought he meant he'd invite some neighbors over someday, if he remembered, and if it was convenient. But he meant the Academy. Next month.

Suddenly my green wool dress was too warm and the plum pastry was doing a crazy ballet in my stomach.

Frau Vogel looked from Herr Hummel to Mutti, bewildered. "Why, that's wonderful! It—it is, isn't it, Anneliese?"

"No, it's not wonderful!" Mutti snapped. "It's the most ridiculous thing I've ever heard. Herr Professor, what are you thinking of?"

My professor replied calmly, "I'm thinking that Greta has an excellent opportunity to play in a recital next month. And that she will need a piano to practice on."

He raised his eyebrows at her, waiting for her answer.

Mutti sighed. "Oh, all *right*! I can't stand up to the three of you! We'll keep the piano."

"Mutti, do you really mean it?" I cried.

"Yes, I mean it!" she snapped. "I said so, didn't I?"

Frau Vogel and I beamed at each other.

"But you must listen to me, Herr Professor," Mutti continued. "You're new in Vienna, so you don't understand the training and skill that are necessary to play at the Academy. I do, because my son played in recitals there. Do you think that Greta is ready—"

"Why don't you ask Greta whether *she* thinks she's ready?" Herr Hummel replied. "If she says no, we'll forget the whole thing."

The three of them looked at me: Mutti angry; Herr Hummel relaxed, waiting; Frau Vogel as round-eyed as a child watching a fairy tale come to life.

"I—I—" In my dreams I was ready to play at the Academy. Why, in my dreams I felt right at home in the Musikverein itself!

But what about in real life? Did I have the courage to try to make my dreams come true?

Herr Hummel thought I did. I couldn't let him down.

I couldn't let myself down.

"Yes," I said. "Yes, I will play in the recital."

On the way home, Mutti walked so fast I had to trot to keep up with her. Her eyes flashed with anger, and her lips were pinched.

"Who is this teacher of yours anyway?" she sputtered. "What do we know about him? Where is he from? Imagine, him pushing you into playing at the Academy!"

"He's not pushing me. I want to play."

Mutti whirled around so quickly I almost ran into her.

"Don't you remember the recitals Kurt used to play in? Remember Elsa, the girl who got a recording contract? And Heinz, the boy Kurt often competed with? *Those* are the kinds of children you'll be performing with—gifted prodigies!"

I didn't say anything. Part of me was furious with Mutti: why couldn't she believe in me, encourage me, the way mothers were supposed to? But part of me thought maybe she was right. I'd never played in public before—and now I had agreed to play in a recital at the Vienna Academy of Music and Performing Arts!

Suddenly I was as shivery as I'd been the time I had the flu.

That night I had a terrible dream. I walked onto a stage in front of thousands of applauding people. I bowed, feeling relaxed and confident. Then I sat down at the piano. But I couldn't remember what I was supposed to play. The music floated down and settled into place in front of me, but I couldn't read it. One impossible passage after another smirked at me from the page. The notes became tiny black bugs that moved and shifted places with one another. "I can't play this!" I whispered to Herr Hummel, who was in the front row. The whisper came out a shout. "She can't play it!" the audience cried. "And she's Kurt Radky's sister!" Everyone laughed. Mutti's voice came from the balcony: "I'm selling her piano after all! She doesn't deserve to keep it!" A man yelled, "Look, she's wearing her nightgown!" I looked down. He was right. Horrified, I tried to run backstage, but I got tangled up in the heavy curtains.

When I woke up, my feather comforter was wrapped tightly around me, just as the velvet curtains in my dream had been. But the sun was shining through my window, and instead of the audience's laughter, I heard the clear, lazy song of the blackbirds and the coo-*COO*-coo of the doves in the courtyard below. From the kitchen came the clinking of cups and Mutti's and Frau Vogel's voices. On Sundays, Frau Vogel went to early mass at the Mariahilfer Church, then stopped at our apartment for coffee and a chat on her way home.

I lay in bed for a while, letting the comfortable Sunday morning noises chase the nightmare away. Then I pulled on an old skirt and sweater and went down the hallway to the kitchen. Along with the cups' clinking, I heard Frau Vogel's voice, full of reproach: "He should have told us what he was planning!" I was afraid she and Mutti were talking about Herr Hummel and the recital, but it was something quite different.

"I don't care *who* runs the government," Mutti was saying as I walked in. "I just don't want to go to war again!"

"War?" I cried, sliding into a chair. "What are you talking about?"

"The latest news," Frau Vogel replied. She poured a cup of coffee and handed it to me. "Eulalie says our Chancellor Schuschnigg has gone to Germany to meet with Herr Hitler this weekend. How do you like that? He says he's going skiing in the Alps, then he sneaks off to a secret meeting with Hitler! I bet you he gives Herr Hitler everything he wants, too."

"As long as we don't go to war, I don't care," Mutti insisted. "Besides, I'm sure there's nothing to worry about." She tapped the open *Wiener Zeitung*—the *Vienna News*—in front of her. "It says right here that the talks between Hitler and Schuschnigg are 'very friendly and are being held in a most cordial atmosphere.' Hitler even met Schuschnigg on the steps of his chalet and greeted him personally."

Frau Vogel snorted. "I'm sure he did! Bullies are always polite and cordial when someone is kissing their—"

"*Hil*de!" Mutti broke in, a shocked little smile on her lips.

I giggled and took a fat braided roll from the bread basket. Our chancellor was quiet and scholarly. With his round eyeglasses and studious face, he looked like a serious young owl. I couldn't imagine him doing what Frau Vogel had started to say!

Frau Vogel lowered her voice. "Anneliese, don't you remember the northern lights?"

A little chill went up my back. Last month, we had seen the northern lights: green gossamer curtains edged with pink; dancing fingers of shimmering white light; faint yellow glows that fluttered and were gone.

I had thought them beautiful, but people had whispered that they were an omen. The last time they were seen in Vienna, people said, was in 1805, right before Napoleon took the city.

"That's just a superstition," Mutti replied with a laugh.

"Maybe so. But if I were you, I'd be looking for a new place to work. Your Herr Rosenwald has been lucky so far, but if the Nazis take over Austria, all Jews will be in danger—and their employees and friends will be, too!"

I gasped. "Mutti, is that true?"

"Certainly not." Mutti dismissed Frau Vogel's fears with a casual wave of her hand. "The Rosenwalds are an old Viennese family. They have money, influence, friends. Why, some of the most important people in Vienna not only shop at their store but are personal friends of theirs! No one would ever let them be abused."

Mutti was right, I thought. The Rosenwalds had Vienna in the palms of their hands. And why not? No one could dislike bustling little Frau Rosenwald with her beautiful brown eyes and ready smile, or her stout husband with his booming laugh. They didn't waltz through life, noses in the air, like most wealthy shop owners; they polka'd through it, stomping and laughing and enjoying themselves enormously. There was nothing they couldn't handle with a good joke, a witty reply, or a clever plan.

Besides, I couldn't worry about the Nazis: I had my recital to worry about. I would have to trust Herr Doctor Schuschnigg—and Frau Vogel—to take care of Austria.

That afternoon I finished all my homework, except for choosing the subject of my essay. Maybe the recital day would be the best day of my life! But maybe it would be the worst. Anyway, I couldn't wait long enough to find out. The essay was due on February twenty-third, ten days from now.

Everybody else had started theirs, I realized when I walked home from school with Annemarie, Paula, Käthe, and Hedi on Monday. Annemarie was writing hers about the day her little brother was born; Paula had chosen the day of her tenth birthday, when her parents took her to the Prater amusement park. Käthe, who was very religious, had chosen her Confirmation Day, and Hedi was writing about a day on her grandparents' farm.

"What are you writing about, Greta?" asked Annemarie.

"I don't know yet," I said.

"You could make up something," Paula suggested.

Hedi's eyes sparkled. "I know! You can write about how the best day of your life was the day you found out you were getting Frau Schäffer for English!"

Everyone shrieked with laughter.

At Mariahilfer Strasse, we split up: Käthe and Hedi to go to Hermann's for pastries, Paula and Annemarie to go to Paula's to study, and I to go home alone.

Perhaps someday I should say, "Everyone's invited to my place!" Frau Vogel would supply me with pastries, and we would study and listen to the radio.

But how awful if they made excuses and didn't come! Or worse, if they came and Mutti was ill and sent them home. That had happened more than once with Erika. We'd come in after school, laughing and talking, to find that Mutti—or, before he died, Kurt—was ill. After a while, Erika and I had started going only to the Brauners'. There we could run and laugh and listen to music, and her parents would just smile.

No, I decided, I wouldn't ask them over. It was safer that way.

Inside our apartment, I threw my book bag and coat onto a chair and sat down to practice. The Mendelssohn and Scarlatti and Schumann beckoned, but I made myself work on the études first. It was like eating leftover boiled beef when you had a chocolate torte sitting in front of you. I did it, though, because I wanted to show Herr Hummel that I could work hard.

The next day after school, I didn't walk home with the other girls. I raced home, grabbed my music, and ran to Herr Hummel's flat. I couldn't wait to hear about the recital! I was hardly inside the door before I started asking questions.

"Herr Professor, when will the recital be? What will I play? Who will be in the audience? How many children will participate?"

Herr Hummel smiled and said, "Sit down on the sofa and have some macaroons while I hang up your coat."

When we'd gotten settled, he said, "The recital will be at the Academy on Friday afternoon, March eleventh, at five o'clock."

"But today is February fifteenth! That's less than a month!"

Herr Hummel held up a hand. "I know. We'll have to select music you can prepare in the little time that's left. But let me begin at the beginning. Perhaps your brother knew Herr Doctor Lothar Haas, who sponsors the recital for young people?"

I nodded, remembering a serious-looking man about Herr Hummel's age with rimless glasses and thinning red hair.

"We were students together in Munich and became friends," Herr Hummel said. "Later he married his sweetheart and they had a little daughter, Liesl. They moved here to Vienna a few years later. Liesl and Lothar's wife both died in the influenza epidemic that hit Vienna after the World War."

I nodded thoughtfully. No wonder I remembered Herr Doctor Haas as always looking sad.

"Liesl was born in March," my professor continued. "So now, because Lothar loves children and misses his little Liesl, he holds a recital every March for ten or so young people who are recommended by their piano teachers. He knows that many children are talented and work hard but need more performing experience than their own teachers can provide for them. Also, the Academy professors come to see who their students of tomorrow may be."

"Are the others very good?" I asked anxiously. "Better than I am?"

He smiled a little. "Many of them will be older than you and will have studied piano longer, but they're not polished performers."

At least I wouldn't be playing with Kurts and Elsas and Heinzes. But one thing still bothered me. "Herr Hummel," I said slowly, "does Herr Doctor Haas want me to play only because I'm Kurt's sister?"

His eyebrows went up the way they did when he was surprised. I was afraid he'd say that it didn't matter why I'd been asked as long as I played well. If he said that, I'd know I'd been right.

But he shook his head. "Come to think of it, I didn't even tell Lothar your name. I merely said I had a promising student I'd like him to hear, and he said you could play in the recital."

"But don't I have to audition or anything? How does he know I'm good enough to play in this recital?"

He shrugged. "Lothar trusts my judgment. Now, come along! My angel and I want to hear you play your études."

After I'd gone through my études and read two new ones, we talked about what I would play for the recital. Herr Hummel thought the Mendelssohn Song Number Six would be a good choice, and I agreed happily. I'd already grown to love it.

"We need another piece, too," he said. "Something livelier, like a sonata or a short waltz."

Of course! My favorite piece, the Scarlatti Sonata in G Major!

Herr Hummel found a copy of it and paced the floor as he listened to me play.

When I'd finished, he nodded. "I think that will be good. We'll start serious work on these two. But I also want you to keep working on your études and scales, and play the pieces I marked in the Bach and Schumann books. If you play only your two recital pieces, they'll become stale. Now, tell me, how much time can you practice every day?"

"Two hours or so most days. I get home from school about two-thirty, and Mutti usually gets home about five. Sometimes she works later, if she has a dress to finish, and I can practice longer. On Sundays it's always been hard. Mutti doesn't tell me *not* to practice, but she keeps sighing and giving me annoyed looks. Or she asks me a million times whether I have homework to do, or she starts talking on the telephone and asks me to be quiet until she's finished."

Herr Hummel thought a minute, drumming his fingers on his chair. Then he said, "Wait a moment!" and went into the kitchen. When he came back, he was clutching something in his hand.

"Here's an extra key to my flat," he said, holding it out to me. "On Sunday afternoons, Lothar and I go have a couple of beers and solve the problems of the world. You are welcome to come practice here during that time—and with your own key, you won't have to ask the building superintendent to let you in."

"Thank you!" I cried, touched. I couldn't think of anything better than a whole afternoon of practicing on Herr Hummel's wonderful piano. "But, Herr Professor, I really must pay you! With money, I mean, not just by practicing. Mutti said she'll give me the money. She said—" I stopped. Mutti had said she didn't want him to think we were even poorer than he was. "Anyway, I want to pay for my lessons."

Herr Hummel shook his head. "I take payment only from wealthy, boring people who have no talent. Tell your mother to let you have the money for something else. Perhaps a new dress for the recital? I know how important clothes are to young girls."

I laughed, but I thought maybe he was right. I might as well go to the recital in a nightgown, the way I did in my dream, as wear any of my too-short, out-of-fashion dresses. Still, it wasn't right for me to use my lesson money for a new dress when Herr Hummel wore old shabby sweaters and the springs in his sofa were ready to pop through the fabric. I wished he weren't so proud!

I thought about it on the way home. Maybe I could give him the money secretly, so he wouldn't know it was from me. I could tuck some Schillings into his coat pocket while his coat was hanging in the entryway, or mail him money in an envelope with no return address. But what if he took his coat to the laundry without checking the pockets, or the money got put in the wrong mailbox?

Suddenly I had it: the Brauners' old desk! I could

leave the money in the secret compartment on Sunday afternoons. Then one day after my lesson, I'd say, "By the way, Herr Professor, did you know that your desk has a secret compartment?" I would show him how to open it—and watch his surprise when he found my Schillings! I wouldn't tell him they were from me. I'd act puzzled and say, "These weren't here when the Brauners left. Erika and I made sure the compartment was empty. Frau Klodzko must have left them. And nobody knows her address, so you'll have to keep the money yourself." The only hard part would be waiting until enough money had built up to make a nice surprise.

Imagining it, I smiled as I climbed the steps to our building.

I checked our little mailbox. Letter for Mutti. Postcard for Mutti. Letter for Mutti. Nothing for me. It had been weeks since I'd heard from Erika. Maybe she'd written and her letter had gotten lost, I told myself. Or maybe she was just busy with that old Rosemary and didn't want to write to me anymore.

I practiced for a while, then left Mutti a note telling her I'd be in the attic. I had nearly finished sorting Kurt's music.

I worked quickly. Beethoven—"B." Liszt—"L." Schumann—"S." Chopin—"C." Mozart—"M." I felt as if I were dancing from the waist up, turning and twisting to put each piece in its proper pile.

Chopin's *Heroic* Polonaise. I fingered the cover gently. Kurt had played that at his last Academy recital, barely a month before he died. I'd held my breath for him through the tricky passages, but he'd done them perfectly. The audience had clapped like crazy as he bowed, and Mutti and I had hugged each other. Afterward we'd gone to Schöner's to celebrate.

I looked up to the ceiling and whispered, "Kurt, are you there? Do you know that now *I'm* going to play at the Academy? I hope you don't mind my doing it when you can't. But it's because you taught me so well that I'm good enough. And I hope you're proud of me."

A loose shutter banged in the wind outside, making me jump, and I felt terribly alone in the dark, dusty attic. I stacked the music back in the trunk. There was still a small pile to be sorted, but I suddenly wanted to go downstairs, where it was light and warm and cozy.

Mutti was in the kitchen, peeling and chopping potatoes and dropping the chunks into a pot of boiling water on the stove beside her.

"Umm, smells like pork roasting." I gave her a kiss on the cheek. "How come you're home so early?"

"Herr Rosenwald told me I could leave. He said it

was because I'd worked extra hours this week, but I think he was afraid I'd strangle Frau Waldmann. She was in five times today, to see that I'm putting the sleeves on her ball gown the way she wants them—and she said she'd stop by again!"

"You should be going to a ball yourself," I told her.

Mutti gave a tired laugh, but I could picture my pretty mother whirling around the dance floor at one of the many balls Vienna held during our Fasching, or winter carnival, season. It didn't seem fair that the closest she got to a ball was the gowns she sewed for women like that great grumpy cow Frau Waldmann.

I sat down at the table and took a macaroon out of the cookie bowl. "Herr Hummel told me all about the piano recital I'm going to play in! It's for children my age, not Academy students or experienced performers. It's to be on Friday, March eleventh, at five o'clock. Herr Hummel said they have to schedule it between our school hours and the Academy's evening concerts. Perhaps we can go to the Sacher for dinner afterward! You'll come, won't you?"

Chop, chop went Mutti's knife on the cutting board. "When did you say it was? March eleventh?"

"Yes, at five o'clock. Please say you'll come!"

Chop, chop, chop. For a terrible second, I was afraid she'd say no.

But she nodded. "I'll be there. I just wish it weren't in March. That's such a busy month at the shop."

She'd never complained about Kurt's recitals being at a busy time, I thought. But at least she'd said she'd come.

"I'm going to play a Scarlatti sonata and one of Mendelssohn's *Songs Without Words*," I said eagerly. "Would you like to hear them after dinner?"

"I'm afraid all I want to do after dinner is go to bed. I'm tired, and my head is achy."

"Oh."

Mutti must have heard the disappointment in my voice, because she looked around at me and added, "I'll listen to them another time, I promise. At any rate, I'll be hearing them at the recital."

For a while, the only sounds were the *chop, chop* of Mutti's knife, the burbling of the water on the stove, and the popping and crackling of the pork roast in the oven.

I finished my macaroon.

"Mutti, are you proud of me?"

"Of course!" She turned around, surprised. "I've always been proud of you. You're polite, and you get good grades and help me with the housework. Speaking of helping me with the housework, would you set the table, please? That's a good girl."

What I had *meant* was, Are you proud of me for playing in a recital at the Academy? But if I had to explain that to her, her answer would mean about as much as the steam rising from the boiling water.

I sighed as I pulled our chipped brown everyday plates out of the kitchen cupboard. Sometimes Mutti seemed even further away than Kurt.

6

The next morning before science class, Elisabeth showed me how to draw a swastika, the zigzaggedy cross that was the Nazis' symbol. It wasn't because I wanted to know how but because she wanted to show off.

"This one sitting," she said, drawing a line that bent like a person sitting. Then she drew a line that bent across the first one. "This one kneeling. Soon you'll see swastikas all over Vienna. They're not illegal anymore. My father says Hitler made Schuschnigg and President Miklas sign an agreement saying so. He also made them put a Nazi in charge of our police and our army, and free all the Nazi prisoners."

That must be why Frau Vogel had called early this morning, I thought. The phone had rung just as I was leaving for school, and I'd heard Mutti say, "The President did what?" and "But, Hilde, if it will avoid a war . . ."

I rolled my eyes and said, "Everybody knows *that*, Elisabeth!"

She said, "Hmmph!" and went to find someone else to pester before Herr Lenski, our science teacher, came in. I heard her giggling as she told Paula Kovacs, "Vater says the Jews are running all over each other trying to get out of Austria in case the Nazis take over. Can't you just see them?"

I thought of our Jewish friends, the Rosenwalds and the Jacobsons. I wanted to pull Elisabeth's perfect golden curls. I wanted to pull them right out of her head.

. . .

On Friday afternoon, when Herr Hummel opened the door, he smiled and cried, "Ah, Greta, my favorite pupil!"

"Your *only* pupil," I teased him.

"And that's the way I want it! Let me turn off the radio," he said, snapping it off as the newscaster was saying, "This morning in Berlin—"

He walked over to his chair by the piano, grumbling, "Sometimes I think I left Germany to come to—to Germany! The Nazis are going to take over all of Europe, and no one will stop them."

He sat down and shook his head sadly. "I'm glad you agreed to play in Lothar's recital this year. I was afraid I might be rushing you a bit, but nobody knows what this year will hold for Austria. If things go badly, this could be the last recital Lothar is able to have."

I nodded as if I understood, but I really didn't. I felt sorry for the Jews and all—but why would politics keep anyone from having a piano recital? It seemed that all the grownups in Vienna were getting as jumpy as Frau Vogel!

Because I couldn't bear to see my professor look so sad, I said, "Guess what! Mutti sold the cupboard to Frau Müller last night and we're definitely keeping the piano! At first Mutti didn't know what to tell the von Prettins, but Frau von Prettin called Wednesday night and bragged about how they could get the Jacobsons' piano for nearly nothing! She said Elisabeth will be taking piano lessons from a man who has taught President Miklas's fourteen children. I wonder whether they have fourteen pianos and all play together."

I was relieved when he chuckled. "I've heard of piano music for four hands—but never piano music for twenty-eight hands! Ah, Greta, you're good for me. No wonder you're my favorite pupil. Now let's hear some piano music for *two* hands!"

Once I'd begun playing, we forgot everything else.

Herr Hummel started to look more like himself as he paced the floor, critiquing my pedaling and giving directions. "Gently here! Put in a slight legato—just slow down a bit for a couple of measures, then go back to tempo. No, don't separate the notes so much. Play them like toes, not fingers; you can put only the tiniest spaces between toes, you know. Why are you laughing?"

"I was thinking of how Schumann would feel if he knew his music reminded you of toes!"

"I'm sure he would understand. Schumann was quite clever. Now start two measures before the legato. Yes, that's better, you're thinking toes now."

When he was finally satisfied with my progress on the Schumann, he had me play both of my recital pieces. I had to start and stop several times, but finally he nodded and said, "They need a bit more work, but I think they'll be in fine shape by March eleventh."

Later, when we were sitting on the sofa, drinking our hot chocolate and eating hunks of dry Christmas cake, I told him about Mutti's saying she'd come to my recital. "I wasn't sure she would, but she said yes. I—I hope she'll be proud of me, the way she and I used to be proud of Kurt when he played."

"Of course she will!" Herr Hummel exclaimed.

"Why wouldn't she be? Unless . . ." He gave me a sharp, mock-suspicious look. "You're not planning to embarrass the poor woman by sticking out your tongue or wiggling your fingers at the audience, are you?"

"No!"

"Kicking Herr Doctor Haas in the shins? Standing on your head and waving your feet in the air?"

"No and *no*!" I giggled.

Herr Hummel folded his arms and looked smug. "Then she will have every reason to be proud of you."

"She said she *is* proud of me, but she didn't mean for my piano playing." I told him what Mutti had said while she was chopping the potatoes. "She just doesn't believe in me."

Herr Hummel nodded sympathetically. "I know she doesn't. I don't understand why that is so, but the reason lies within her troubled mind, not within you. And you know that there are people who do believe in you."

"You do," I said shyly.

He nodded. "You're right. I do, very much. Can you tell me who else believes in you?"

"Frau Vogel."

"Yes, she does. Who else?"

"Kurt would if he were here. So would Erika."

"You're right," Herr Hummel agreed. "But there's someone else I'm waiting for you to mention. Someone very important."

I licked my forefinger and used it to pick up cake crumbs off the plate while I thought. "Herr Doctor Haas? He must believe in me to let me play in the recital without even hearing me."

"Yes, he does. But I'm thinking of someone even more important."

More important than Herr Doctor Haas?

I licked the crumbs off my finger as I thought some more. Then something shiny caught my eye.

"The angel!"

Herr Hummel laughed. "Of course the angel believes in you! But what about *you*—Anna Margareta Radky? Do you believe in yourself?"

Surprised, I shrugged and said, "I—I guess so!"

He wagged a forefinger at me. "You must be *sure* that you believe in yourself—not just when you play music, but all the time! I want you to think about it. That will be part of your assignment, along with the études and the recital pieces."

I did think about it after I got home, while I was sorting music in the attic. Kurt had believed in himself. I'd never seen him nervous before a recital or an audition. He'd always been confident with people, too; he'd signed tons of autographs and laughed and talked with everyone. He'd known just what to say to the old women to make them feel younger, and to the young girls to make them feel older.

But what about me? Even thinking about the upcoming recital made my heart race and my stomach churn. And I was too shy to try to become better friends with the girls at school. So maybe I *didn't* believe in myself.

On the other hand, if I truly didn't believe in myself, I wouldn't have agreed to play at the Academy. I sighed and tossed a book of Clementi sonatas onto the "C" pile.

That evening, while I was studying my German grammar, Mutti said, "By the way, I'm having my bridge club over Sunday afternoon. We were going to Ilse's but Josef wants to listen to a speech Herr Hitler is giving on the radio. I thought perhaps I could tell her to bring Elisabeth, and the two of you could—"

"I can't," I said quickly. "I'm going to Herr Hummel's on Sunday."

"That's too bad," Mutti said. "I thought perhaps now, with Erika gone, you'd be lonely."

"I am, but . . ." It wouldn't help to explain. Mutti thought Elisabeth was darling.

. . .

On Sunday afternoon, I helped Mutti clean the apartment and put the little cakes from Hermann's on a tray. I escaped with an armload of music as Mutti's friends were coming in.

At first, Herr Hummel's living room seemed silent and strange with only me there. But once I started playing, it was lovely having that piano and the whole afternoon to practice!

The longer I played, the more the piano seemed an extension of myself, instead of a separate thing that I moved my fingers on. The melodies flowed smoothly from my hands, spinning out a prelude or a sonata.

Finally I stopped to rest.

Perhaps I should put my Schillings into the old desk now, I thought, in case Herr Hummel came home early. I got them out of my coat pocket. "Don't tell!" I whispered to the angel.

It was fun to press the tiny brass button and see the false bottom pop up, just the way it always had. But then I groaned with disappointment. A German passport and an envelope stared up at me from the hidden compartment. Herr Hummel was already using it!

I glanced into the passport to make sure it was his.

"Hummel, Wilhelm," it said, and showed a photo of him looking somber.

Perhaps Frau Vogel had told him about the desk's little compartment. Once, when Frau and Herr Brauner were out and their maid Clara was sick, she had stayed with Erika and me and we'd shown her how to press the button and make it open.

I scowled. What should I do with my Schillings? Finally, I tucked them inside Herr Hummel's passport. Maybe he would think he'd put them there and forgotten them. And if I did have to confess that I'd done it myself, it wouldn't be so bad. After all, I hadn't seen anything really private—just his passport and an envelope. But it would have been so much more fun the way I'd planned it!

"Herr Professor?" came Frau Vogel's voice, along with a *tap-tap* on the door.

I quickly shut the desk and ran to the door.

Frau Vogel exclaimed, "Greta! I didn't know you were here."

I explained about Herr Hummel's loaning me his extra key. "Would you like to leave him a note?"

"No, it's not important. He asked me to tell him what Adolf Hitler had to say on the radio this afternoon. It was the first time Radio Vienna has broadcast one of his speeches, you know. Well"—she waved her hand in scorn—"I can assure the professor that he didn't miss a thing. Nearly three hours that speech lasted! And what did the great Hitler talk about? German productivity! How much each factory is producing for the Fatherland, how much each farm district is producing for the Fatherland. Pah! I was surprised he didn't tell us how many kittens each loyal German cat is producing for the Fatherland!"

I laughed. "Would you like to come in and hear what I'll be playing in the recital?"

"Oh, yes!" Frau Vogel beamed with pleasure.

She sat down on the sofa, her back very straight and her hands folded in her lap, as though she were waiting for a concert of the Vienna Philharmonic to begin.

I wasn't ready to play from memory yet, so I opened my Scarlatti. I thought of pretending that this was the recital, that a hundred professors and parents were listening to me, but the thought made my heart pound and my hands stiff. Better just to see dear Frau Vogel, with her flowered apron and unruly gray hair.

I played both pieces well. When I'd finished, Frau Vogel clapped until I was afraid her hands would fall off.

"Bravo!" she cried. "That was lovely! Your mother will be so proud of you at the recital."

I replied sadly, "I don't think she wants to come."

"That mother of yours!" Frau Vogel rolled her eyes. "She should be *pleased* to have another pianist in the family. I've told her that over and over, but she just frowns."

"Frau Vogel, can I tell you something? Sometimes I think—I think Mutti just loved Kurt more. I know he was sick and needed a lot of care, but sometimes I think—" I couldn't bring myself to say the words: Mutti would rather *I'd* died instead of Kurt.

Frau Vogel clucked her tongue sympathetically and said, "Oh, lovey, I'm sure that's not true! Your mother loves you very much. But I could tell you that all day, and it's *her* you need to hear it from, isn't it?" She patted my hand and said resolutely, "I'll talk to her. I'll let her know how you feel."

Reluctantly, I shook my head. "Thank you, but I have to be the one to talk to her about it."

Frau Vogel hugged me. "I suppose you're right. But let me know if I can help." She gave me a big kiss in the middle of my forehead. "Now I must get back upstairs and take my little tea cakes out of the oven. I made them for Helga Müller, since she's ill with the flu."

I followed her to the door.

"Frau Vogel, do you remember that little desk over

there? The one Erika and I used to play with? Did you show Herr Hummel how to open the secret compartment?"

She stopped and thought. "Yes. Yes, I did. I came down to bring him a cake—or was it a fruit torte? No, it was my best chocolate-raspberry cake. He was working at that desk, and I showed him how to push the little button." She leaned forward conspiratorially and whispered, "I thought he might have things to hide, with him maybe having a Past and all!"

"You mean love letters?" I had to press my lips together to keep from laughing.

She nodded solemnly. "Love letters, photos, jewels, secret codes! You never know, when someone shows up suddenly with only a suitcase, the way he did! Now, if he were Jewish, I'd think he just got run out of Germany. But he's not Jewish! I asked him, and he said no, that his family was Catholic. Now I really must go! Bye-bye, lovey!"

After Frau Vogel left, I began practicing again. Finally, when it started to get dark in the flat, I stood up and stretched. My arms ached from all the music that had flowed through them. It had been a marvelous day, though, one of the best in a long time. *One of the best* . . . I stopped in the middle of a stretch, my arms still high above my head. I could write about today for my essay on the best day of my life!

After dinner that night, I settled down on the sofa with my notebook and a German–English dictionary. Writing the essay was hard work, even after all that extra English study with Erika.

When I'd finished the first draft, I read it over. Frau Schäffer would like it, I thought. She had said she would read the essays aloud so we could learn from everyone's mistakes. I didn't think I'd made any mistakes—but would the other girls laugh at what I'd written? "Greta Radky's favorite day was one she spent all by herself!" they might say. "We knew she was odd, but imagine her sitting alone, practicing the piano all day, and *liking* it! What did Erika ever see in her?"

Actually, I hadn't been alone all day. Frau Vogel had come down, and it *had* been nice to take a break and talk to someone. I inserted, "A friend came to visit me. We talked, and she listened to me play." If anyone asked who it was, I'd say, "Oh, she doesn't go to school here." That wouldn't be a lie.

I still needed a few more lines to make the essay two pages long, as it was supposed to be.

I could say I was going to be playing in a recital at the Academy! But did I want everybody to know about that? What if I was a flop and didn't want anyone asking me about it afterward?

Then, clear as anything, I heard Herr Hummel's

voice in my head. "But what about *you*—Anna Margareta Radky? Do you believe in yourself?"

I guessed I wasn't believing in myself very much if I was so afraid of failing that I kept the recital a secret.

I took a deep breath and wrote, "My professor asked me to play at the Vienna Academy of Music and Performing Arts on March eleventh. I said yes. I was very excited that he asked me."

There! I was believing in myself and using a lot of past-tense verbs. Herr Hummel and Frau Schäffer should both be happy.

I copied over the essay in ink and tucked it carefully into my notebook, ready to be turned in the next day.

7

That night I dreamed that Frau Vogel called and said, "Greta, the *Wiener Zeitung* says you have no friends and do nothing but sit alone and practice the piano. All Vienna is talking about how strange you are! What's more, people are placing bets on whether you'll do well at the recital."

The dream was so real it was a relief the next morning to see that the headlines were about Herr Hitler, not me.

After school I had two surprises. The first was a postcard from Erika with a skyscraper on the front. In tiny letters, she'd written:

Today Rosemary's dad took us to see the Empire State Building. It is 102 stories high! Tonight we're going to see Snow White, *a new cartoon movie.*

New York City is so big, it makes Vienna look like a pokey little village. Still, I get homesick! I miss you! Erika

I felt some jealous pangs at the parts about Rosemary. But at least Erika had written, and she'd said she missed me. I stuck the postcard in the corner of my mirror, and, after practicing, I wrote her back. I told her about Herr Hummel and the recital and my essay and everything else I could think of. I told her that everyone missed her, but nobody as much as I did.

The second surprise came when Mutti got home that evening. She handed me a parcel wrapped in brown paper. "This is for you. See if you like it."

I pulled off the twine and pushed back the paper. Nestled in white tissue was a folded length of silk crepe in a deep, beautiful sapphire blue.

I gasped. "I love it!"

Mutti was taking off her boots. "Frau Neumann ordered it and then fell in love with a rose silk, and couldn't afford both. She decided on the rose, and Herr Rosenwald said I could have this. I thought you could use a new dress."

The fabric was as soft and cool as water as it flowed through my hands. It even smelled sweet and delicate. I knew that was Frau Rosenwald's perfume, which you could often smell in the shop, but the scent seemed to come from the fabric itself.

"It's gorgeous! Mutti, could you finish it in time for my recital? Please! I can't wear my old green wool. It's too tight across the—well, under the arms."

"I know." Mutti's eyes went to my chest. "We need to make our trip to Gerngross pretty soon, don't we?"

Gerngross was the big department store across from the Mariahilfer Church. Mutti had been planning to take me there to get my first bra. I was dreading it, but I *had* to have a recital dress from that beautiful crepe; if it meant trying on bras under the eye of a snooty saleslady, I'd do it.

"We can go next week," I said.

Mutti considered. "When is your recital? March eleventh? And today is February twenty-first. All right. I think I can do it."

"Thank you, Mutti! I'll be the best-dressed pianist there."

"Well, if you insist on playing in this recital, I want you to be nicely dressed."

After dinner we planned my dress. It was to have a softly flared skirt with unpressed pleats across the front (Mutti said that was the newest style in America), and a sash around the waist. The sleeves would be full, caught by narrow cuffs. At the neckline I would wear a lace jabot of Mutti's; she would take tucks in it to make it smaller, and sew a tiny sapphire-colored bow in it.

For the recital I'd wave my hair with Mutti's curling iron. I'd wear it with the front pulled back into the gold-filigree clasp Frau Vogel had given me for

Christmas. I'd been saving it for a special occasion.

I hugged myself with excitement. The recital was taking on shapes and sounds and colors. When I thought of it now, I could see how I'd look as well as hear how I'd sound.

The only thing I didn't know was how I'd feel, playing in a room full of people watching and listening and judging me. I wouldn't know that until I began to play.

• • •

"Your memorization is coming along well," Herr Hummel said when I played the Scarlatti and Mendelssohn for him the next evening.

I nodded. "I didn't *try* to memorize them. I've just played them so much that I can do it better without the music now. But, Herr Professor, what if I'm so nervous at the recital that I forget the notes?"

He said merrily, "Then I shall yell 'It's a G-minor chord, Greta!' at the top of my lungs, and everyone will laugh."

"I won't laugh."

"I know, but once you start playing, you won't forget the notes either. Your fingers will remember them. Greta, I know it's your first recital," he added, smiling gently, "but you must give the music in you a chance to chase away the fear, instead of letting the fear chase away the music. Do you understand?"

I nodded. "That sounds like part of believing in myself."

"It is, exactly. And the music is so strong within you I am sure it will have the fear running all the way to the ocean!"

After I'd finished playing through some new études, Herr Hummel had a surprise for me. My third surprise in two days!

"Saturday afternoon, I'm going to my favorite music store. If you're free after school, I'll wait for you. I would like you to come along and meet Herr Ornstein, who owns the shop. Afterward we shall stop for pastries and coffee, like good Viennese. Can you come?"

I nodded happily. "I'd love to!"

When I told Mutti about our plan, she frowned.

"I suppose you can go," she said reluctantly. "But I think you're spending a lot of time with that professor of yours."

I just shrugged and didn't answer.

• • •

At my lesson on Friday, Herr Hummel and I finalized our plans. Saturday afternoon we walked to the corner to catch the streetcar. As we rode toward the Ring, the elegant boulevard that encircled central Vienna, Herr Hummel told me about the music shop we were going to.

"Jacob Ornstein used to be one of the finest cellists in Germany," he said. "He performed in Berlin for many years, then played and taught here in Vienna before the arthritis in his hands got too bad. His music shop is small and plain, but it's one of the best I know of."

We got off the streetcar near St. Stephan's Cathedral and walked down Rotenturmstrasse into the Jewish sector. Herr Ornstein's shop was on a quiet, narrow, brick-paved street, where dark old buildings closed in on us from both sides.

When Herr Hummel opened the music-shop door, a little bell tinkled and a man's voice cried, "I will be right with you!"

I immediately felt at home in the tiny shop. It was tidy and snug, with the smell of fresh coffee and sweet pipe tobacco. Glass cases with instruments filled the center of the room. File cabinets lined both of the long walls; above them hung dozens of framed photos of musicians. From behind the counter, a Victrola played a Haydn string quartet.

"That's Herr Ornstein's old Berlin quartet," Herr Hummel told me, nodding toward the record. "I used to go to their performances, but I didn't meet Herr Ornstein until I came here."

I nodded, my ear picking out the lowest line of the

four intertwining melodies. Herr Ornstein's cello spoke nobly and gently.

Ffffrrip! The green curtain at the back of the shop was pushed aside, and a very tall, thin man with a mop of white hair walked through.

"Ah, Herr Professor Hummel!" he cried, taking long strides toward us. "My best customer!"

"And Herr Ornstein, my favorite shopkeeper. How are you?"

They shook hands and clasped arms the way men do when they haven't seen each other for a long time.

"Hello, Fräulein." Herr Ornstein smiled at me.

I curtsied and murmured, "*Küss die Hand.*"

Herr Hummel said, "This is my student, Greta. She is going to play in her first piano recital soon, at the Academy."

"Ahhh!" Herr Ornstein's bushy white eyebrows went up. "At the Academy! You must be a very good pianist indeed, Fräulein. Please come back to my shop often."

While the two men searched for the music Herr Hummel wanted, I went to look at the gallery of photos over the far cabinets. Most were of Viennese musicians: principals of the Vienna Philharmonic, the Vienna Symphony, and the Vienna Opera Company; Bruno Walter, Wilhelm Furtwängler, Hans Knappertsbusch, and other well-known conductors; opera singers Richard Tauber and Anton Dermota; soloists who'd performed in Vienna, such as—

Kurt. Kurt in his formal concert dress, sitting at a piano and looking at the photographer with grave eyes and a soft smile. I remembered that photo. It had been taken when Kurt won the Young Viennese Pianist Award. We had had a copy of it in the living room before he died.

I stared at the photo. Kurt looked so alive, so real, I could almost hear his voice.

My cheeks were wet before I even knew I was crying. I wiped them with the back of my hand, quickly, before anyone could see.

Herr Ornstein went into the back room to answer the telephone, and my teacher came over to me. He followed my gaze and saw the autograph on the photo. "Ah, your brother!"

I nodded and swallowed the lump in my throat. "It's the first time I've seen his picture since he died. Mutti locked them all away. I wish—"

I stopped and bit my lip. I had started to say, "I wish you'd known him." But I'd realized suddenly that it wasn't true. I was glad Herr Hummel *hadn't* known Kurt!

The thought made me feel shaky and dizzy, as if the floor had opened up under me. How could I be so selfish as to be glad Herr Hummel hadn't known Kurt? I'd loved Kurt!

But the thought had already formed itself in my mind and I couldn't un-form it: Herr Hummel was the only person who'd ever been *mine*. Kurt had had everybody else: Mutti, the professors at the Academy, and all those adoring fans who'd squealed over everything from his playing of Schumann to his chestnut curls.

Of course I'd been glad he had admirers and happy times; they'd helped make up for the pain and the awful times. But was it so wrong to want someone of my own?

Herr Hummel patted my shoulder and handed me his handkerchief.

"I'm sorry," he said quietly. "I never realized his picture was here. I wouldn't have brought you if I had known."

"It's all right."

Herr Ornstein came back, and the two men continued looking through the file cabinets. I tried to look at music, too, but my eyes kept going back to the photo of Kurt. If only he could step out of the picture and we could be together, even for a few minutes!

I was glad when Herr Hummel called me over and began to explain the differences between two editions of a Beethoven piano concerto.

After they had found all the music on my professor's list, he chose a few other purchases and paid Herr Ornstein.

"Best of luck at your recital, Fräulein," Herr Ornstein called as we left.

"Thank you, and I shall come back to your shop," I replied.

As we walked back up Rotenturmstrasse, my professor asked, "Are you all right now? After seeing your brother's picture?"

"No. Yes. I don't know!" My feelings were like the northern lights: swirling, changing, some of them flickering so faintly they were gone before I could catch them. Then, without knowing I was going to, I blurted out, "Kurt was so ill, he hurt so much, and I couldn't do anything! I couldn't make the pain go away! And he *died*, and I couldn't do anything!"

"I know you couldn't," Herr Hummel said quietly. "You can never do enough about other people's suffering, no matter how much you love them and want to help. But you mustn't feel guilty." He hesitated, then said, "I know all about guilt feelings. Before I moved here, I—well, I tried to help a lot of people. I did help many of them, but I couldn't reach them all. And there were some I helped but couldn't save in the end."

"Do you mean the Jews in Germany?"

He nodded slowly. "The Jews and some others. I used to see their faces in my mind every day, the ones I couldn't save. I had to tell myself many, many times that I had done all I could. And you must tell yourself the same thing about your brother—you loved him and helped care for him, and that was all you could do."

It was strange. If someone had asked me whether I felt guilty about Kurt's dying, I would have said, "No, it wasn't my fault!" But now, suddenly, I felt lighter, as if someone had taken a chunk of lead from my heart.

Herr Hummel said, "Let's find a place to have our coffee and sweets. We both need something to cheer us up a bit."

We walked down the Graben, one of Vienna's main avenues, and turned onto busy Kohlmarkt. Vienna looked festive today, probably because of the rousing speech Chancellor Schuschnigg had made on Thursday evening. Mutti and I had listened to it on the radio. "Austria has made all the concessions to Germany it is going to make!" he had pronounced. "It is time to say, 'This far and no further!' Austria will never voluntarily give up its independence!" The crowd had gone mad with cheering. Now long banners that looked like Austria's flag—two bands of red with a band of white in between—hung from many stores and government buildings in Vienna. Some of the buildings' walls sported the painted words RED-WHITE-RED! and *HEIL*, AUSTRIA!

Herr Hummel was turning toward a café with white awnings and a big gold crest over the door.

"Let's stop here, at Demel," he said. "I hear it has the best pastries in all Vienna. Except for Frau Vogel's, that is!"

"Demel is—uh, rather expensive," I told him, thinking of his used furniture and shabby sweaters.

He misunderstood. "It's all right. I'm treating you."

"But—" Then I stopped. I didn't want to hurt his pride. I'd put some extra Schillings into the old desk instead.

As we went in, a white-aproned waitress curtsied and greeted us. I felt like a grownup.

The pastry counter was on our left. We gazed in awe at the array of pastries on their crystal trays and silver pedestal servers: flaky golden strudels; little custard tarts topped with glazed strawberries; tall pink cakes; chocolate tortes with layers of jam and cake under brittle, shiny icing; crepes filled with chestnut cream; cakes with layers of chocolate and almond-green filling; and all kinds of iced sweet rolls.

Herr Hummel decided on a custard-and-strawberry tart. I was trying to decide between the chestnut crepes and a slice of chocolate torte when a strange thing happened. A man came out of the next room, started to squeeze past us, then stopped and stared at Herr Hummel. He was young, maybe a few years older than Kurt would have been. He was only a little taller than I was, and had close-cropped brown hair and gold-rimmed glasses.

"Well," he said slowly, "if it isn't the great—"

"Good afternoon," Herr Hummel broke in curtly. "Herr Rudolf Beck, is it not?"

"So you remember me!" Herr Beck smiled, but it was a nasty, smirky smile. He drew himself up as if trying to seem taller than he was. "I'm flattered! But I may be Herr *Professor* Beck soon. I'm here to see about a position at the Horak Conservatory." He gave a phony little laugh.

"Why," he continued, "I'm surprised that no one has contacted you about it, Herr Maestro! Isn't the faculty at the Conservatory aware that such a great pianist is in Vienna?"

His voice was insulting, his eyes mocking.

"I am retired," Herr Hummel replied quietly. Then he looked at me and said, "Go and find us a table. If you don't, we may wait all night for a place to sit."

I quickly ordered a slice of chocolate torte and sat down at a little round marble table in the next room. There were plenty of empty tables! Herr Hummel had just wanted to get rid of me. But why?

I could see my professor and Herr Beck through the glass shelves with knickknacks beside me. Herr Hummel was stiff and unsmiling, and Rudolf Beck was smirking and laughing. Their voices reached me, but I couldn't hear what they were saying.

Finally Herr Beck went out the door with another fake laugh. Herr Hummel came over to our table, looking shaken.

"Who was that man?" I asked before he'd even sat down.

He gestured impatiently. "Just a silly boy. Forget you saw him. Hmmph, the Horak Conservatory indeed! He's even more arrogant than I thought if he thinks they'll have him there."

An arrogant young pianist.

"Is he the one you dreamed about? Remember, when I came to my first lesson? You had dreamed about a student of yours from Munich."

Herr Hummel thought. "Yes, it was Herr Beck. I'd forgotten about that dream. He wasn't a student of mine, though. He wanted to be, but I wouldn't have him." Then Herr Hummel began grumbling to himself again. "Hmmph! Insolent puppy! Should have been drowned at birth!"

Our waitress came with our orders. I asked her to bring me a *Melange*, which was half coffee and half steamed milk. Herr Hummel asked for a large cup of black coffee.

The *Melange* and chocolate torte were wonderful! I ate slowly, savoring each bite.

Herr Hummel attacked his tart fiercely with his fork.

I giggled. "You're supposed to eat it, not murder it!"

Herr Hummel smiled. "I'm sorry. I just hadn't expected to meet Rudolf Beck in Vienna. The last time I saw him—except in the dream—was long ago, in my studio in Munich."

"Herr Professor, where did you teach? At the Conservatory in Munich?"

I hoped he'd say yes. That would give me a good answer for Mutti the next time she asked what his qualifications were.

But my professor was shaking his head. "I never taught at a school, only privately." Then he laughed. "I remember when Beck came to play for me. He had been hounding me to give him lessons, and I had refused him over and over. You see, I could tell just from the way he talked that he would be an arrogant, impatient student. The type of musician who—how shall I say it?—who uses music to present his skill to the world instead of using his skill to present the music. Do you understand?"

I wasn't sure I did, but I nodded so that he would go on with his story.

"I finally agreed to listen to Beck play," Herr Hummel continued. "His performance was just what I had expected. He played Scriabin's Etude Number Three, which is very dramatic and discordant. He played it horribly, tossing his head, twisting his body, and making the chords crash like thunder. When he was finished, he stood up and bowed and said, 'There! What do you think of that?' I said, 'Herr Beck, if you want only to gyrate dramatically in front of a large audience, why don't you become a traffic policeman? Then no one will have to *listen* to you while you do it.' "

"You *didn't*! What did he say to that?"

Herr Hummel shrugged. "He packed up his music and stomped out of my apartment, making noises about how he'd get even with me someday."

I had a lot more questions to ask him, but he set down his empty coffee cup and said, "Now, if you are finished, we'd better be getting home. I'll try to forget about Rudolf Beck. Such people are not worth worrying about."

But he was quiet and preoccupied the whole way home, and I knew that he wasn't forgetting Herr Beck for one minute.

8

The next day, Sunday, I got ready to go to Herr Hummel's to practice again.

Mutti frowned when I told her where I was going. "I still think you ought to be spending more time with other girls your age," she said. "As a matter of fact, there's a new saleslady at Rosenwald's who just moved here from Innsbruck with her husband and children. Her name is Irmgarde Siegler, and she has a daughter your age who will be going to your school as soon as they get settled. Perhaps I could tell Irmgarde to send her over sometime."

I shook my head. "No, Mutti. I'm busy practicing for my recital."

"But it wouldn't hurt for you to be friendly!" Mutti sounded impatient. "Irmgarde says she's very shy, and they live just a few blocks away."

"I'm too busy right now." I got my books from the piano bench and left without saying more. I hated it when Mutti tried to make friends for me!

Before I began to practice, I greeted the little angel and put my week's allowance into the secret compartment of the desk.

As on the Sunday before, I practiced for hours. First, of course, I worked on my recital pieces. I didn't need to look at the music at all now when I played them. They flowed naturally. I didn't think about how I moved my fingers any more than I would think about how I moved my mouth when I talked.

Next I opened my étude book to the pages Herr Hummel had assigned me on Friday. The two horrid-looking études bared their teeth, daring me to try them. I had to go through them very slowly several times. It took me over an hour to play them smoothly and up to tempo. Afterward I rewarded myself by playing pieces from the Bach and Schumann books, just because I loved being part of that music. Finally, when it began to get dark, I closed the piano lid, said goodbye to the angel, and walked home.

"I was about to call Frau Vogel to go down and see about you," Mutti said crossly when I came in. "Didn't your professor know you'd need to come home and eat dinner?"

"I'm sorry, Mutti," I said. I hadn't told Mutti that Herr Hummel wasn't there on Sunday afternoons. I was afraid she'd say, "You have no business being there alone!" and stop me from going.

The following afternoon, my heart beat a little faster as we prepared for English class. Frau Schäffer had said on Saturday that she'd read our essays out loud today. "Most of them were very good," she'd said, "and I found out some interesting things about a few of you." I was sure she'd looked at me when she said that.

But the essays didn't get read on Monday, because Frau Schäffer had been called away to Linz to care for her father. We had a substitute, a very young, new teacher named Herr Nordheim.

"Wasn't he adorable?" Hedi giggled as we walked home from school.

Paula sighed dreamily. "I wish we had him all the time."

"Maybe Frau Schäffer will have to move back to Linz," Annemarie said excitedly, "and he'll teach us permanently."

Käthe said, "I have an announcement to make: I am no longer even *thinking* of becoming a nun!"

Everyone laughed. As usual, I couldn't think of anything to say. I had thought Herr Nordheim was nice, but very young and scared-looking, not at all handsome or romantic.

Not at all like Herr Hummel, I found myself thinking. Then, when I realized I'd thought that, I blushed so furiously I had to fake a coughing fit to cover it up. Herr Hummel wasn't handsome or romantic either, but he was the most wonderful person I'd ever met. Did I have a crush on him? Maybe. But if having a crush on someone meant you had to talk out loud about how dreamy he was and how cute he looked when he scrunched up his nose (as Annemarie was saying now about Herr Nordheim), I guessed I didn't. Just the thought of saying things like that about Herr Hummel made me blush again.

"Are you all right?" Käthe asked, turning around.

"I'm fine," I said. I trotted to catch up with her and the others. "But I have to turn here at the corner to meet Mutti. We're going to Gerngross to do some shopping. Bye!"

"Bye, Greta!" they called.

I was glad they didn't ask what Mutti and I were going to shop for. I would sooner have eaten my book bag than said, "A bra," out loud in public.

The bra-buying wasn't as bad as I'd thought it would be. I did feel a little cowed by the tidy saleslady, with her neat bun and plucked, arched eyebrows. When she looked me over haughtily and said, "And what size do we take, Fräulein?" I could only stammer in confusion.

But Mutti took care of her neatly. "I'm a designer at Rosenwald's," she said politely but firmly. "I prefer to do the fitting myself. I'll call you if there's a problem." Then it was the saleslady's turn to stammer, since every woman in Vienna was impressed by the name Rosenwald's.

Mutti knew how to check each tiny detail of each bra's fit and construction. When we found one that met her approval, she bought it and two others just like it so I'd have extras.

We left the store with me wearing one of the bras. I felt as if I had a sign on me that said, LOOK! GIRL WEARING FIRST BRA!

"For goodness' sake, don't hunch over like that," Mutti whispered.

"I can't help it," I whispered back, growing red. My chest seemed to stick out at least twice as far as it had before. I was glad when we got outside and I could button my coat over the new rise and fall in my school jumper.

"I need to stop at the butcher shop," Mutti said. "Then we can have coffee and cakes at Hermann's, if you'd like."

"I would." I nodded happily. I couldn't remember when Mutti and I had last gone shopping and stopped for a treat.

While Mutti was inside the butcher shop, I strolled

up and down Mariahilfer Strasse, looking idly in shop windows. I hoped Mutti wouldn't be long. It was getting cold, even with my coat—

"Well, it's the little girl from Demel," a voice behind me said.

I turned around, startled. It was Rudolf Beck. Even his voice made chills go up my back.

"There must be something very interesting in the window of that bookshop. What is it, Fräulein?"

"It's nothing," I murmured. My heart was pounding. I didn't want to talk to Rudolf Beck. I didn't trust him. But I couldn't go into the butcher shop and get Mutti, because he was standing between me and the shop door.

"You're not afraid of me, are you?" He was smirking at me just as he had at Herr Hummel. "I was hoping you would help me. I need to talk to your piano professor. I believe he lives in this area. Perhaps you can tell me where."

I shook my head. "No. I—I don't know where he lives."

"But don't you go to his apartment for your lessons?"

I was trembling now. How did he know I took lessons from Herr Hummel? "He—he moved away. I don't know where!"

I ran past him and got to the door of the butcher shop just as Mutti was coming out.

"Greta, who was that man? What did he want with you?"

I made a quick decision. If I told Mutti about Rudolf Beck, she might think Herr Hummel was involved in something dangerous and not want me to see him anymore.

"Oh, he was just lost and asked for directions." I hoped I sounded casual.

"Then how come you're walking so fast?"

"Because I'm hungry!"

I didn't even feel like having coffee and cakes now, but I had to pretend I did. I had to convince Mutti that everything was all right. Besides, I didn't want Rudolf Beck to follow us home. It would be best if we went to Hermann's and stayed until he was certain to be gone.

I was still trembling when the waiter brought our raspberry tarts and coffee.

"Are you sure you're all right?" Mutti was looking at me closely. "Your hands are shaking. Greta, tell me the truth! If that man was bothering you, we should tell the police."

I shook my head. "I *told* you, he wanted directions to—to the subway. He just startled me, was all. And my hands were shaking because I was cold. See? I'm fine now."

Mutti didn't look convinced, but she didn't say any more.

Why *did* Rudolf Beck want to see Herr Hummel? Maybe he just wanted to brag that he'd gotten the position at the Horak Conservatory. Or maybe he wanted to talk Herr Hummel into taking a job there.

It's probably nothing to worry about, I told myself as I ate my tart. I'd tell Herr Hummel about it at my lesson tomorrow.

• • •

The next morning, I tried to sneak off to school without my bra, but Mutti made me go back and put it on. It was itchy and tight. If Erika were here, I thought, we could laugh about it and I'd feel all right. But writing to her about it just wouldn't be the same.

That afternoon, we had a new substitute for Frau Schäffer—a large, no-nonsense woman named Frau Fischer. She had thin lips that never curved in a smile. To the other girls' huge disappointment, she announced that she would be with us until Frau Schäffer came back. Herr Nordheim was starting a permanent job at a boys' academy across town.

"What a waste!" I heard Hedi grumble.

Mutti's co-worker's daughter, Lore Siegler, started

school that day. She reminded me of a little sparrow: short, slender, and plain, with unremarkable eyes and straight light-brown hair cut at chin level.

When our teachers introduced her, she just ducked her head and blushed.

"She looked terrified," Hedi said on our way home that afternoon. "Did she think we were going to eat her or something?"

Käthe added, "I tried to talk to her, but she barely answered me. I feel sorry for her."

I nodded in agreement. Lore had looked miserable all day. I might have asked her to walk home from school with me if Mutti hadn't tried to push me into being friends with her.

As soon as I got to Herr Hummel's, I told him about meeting Rudolf Beck on Mariahilfer Strasse. His eyebrows met in the middle as I talked.

"Thank you for letting me know."

"But what does he want with you?" I asked.

"Oh, he's angry because he found out he didn't get the position he applied for at the Conservatory. Lothar talked to a friend who teaches there. He said Beck seemed to think I have influence at that school and had told the director not to hire him. What a fool he is! He must always find someone to blame besides himself."

"He can't do anything to hurt you, can he?"

Herr Hummel shook his head. "If he were staying here, he would probably harass me. As it is, he's going back to Munich tomorrow. One of Lothar's friends is taking him and some other job candidates to the train station in the morning. I doubt that we'll ever hear of him again. I'm only sorry he frightened you. Now let's forget that silly boy and listen to your études."

I played my études, but I had the feeling that Herr Hummel's mind was elsewhere, and I wanted to know where. Maybe, I thought, it was time to try asking him again—delicately—about his Past. So after my lesson, while we were having our hot chocolate, I asked, "Herr Hummel, why did you leave Munich?"

He looked at me, startled. He thought a minute, then asked *me* a question. "How much do you know about the Nazis?"

"Not very much," I replied. I told him the things I'd heard: that they hated the Jews, that Hitler was a madman who wouldn't stop until he ruled the world, that everybody had to do everything he said. "But some of my teachers say the Nazis would protect us from the Communists. And Mutti says they would wipe out the poverty and unemployment in Vienna."

Herr Hummel smiled grimly. "They would wipe out a few other things as well—creativity, human decency, and the entire Jewish race. Do you remember Herr Ornstein, the music-shop owner? He was a fine cellist, but he had to stop playing in Germany even before his arthritis got bad. The Nazis declared that Jewish musicians could no longer perform or teach there."

I nodded thoughtfully. I'd heard of that cruel, silly rule.

"Living under the Nazis is your worst nightmare." Herr Hummel leaned forward and looked at me intently. "They're every bit as bad as the Communists. You must agree with everything they say and support everything they do. You are watched and spied upon, perhaps even by your best friends. And the Nazis destroy anything that does not fit their image of perfect Germans. They burn books that show other ways of life, they ban music and art that do not glorify Nazi Germany, and they discard human beings who are not of pure German ancestry."

His words frightened me. Still, this wasn't Germany, it was Austria—and surely we'd never let those things happen here! I was more interested in hearing about Herr Hummel.

"Is that why you left Germany, because you didn't want to live under the Nazis? Or did you have to—well, escape?"

"Let's say that I left very quietly because I had

some trouble with the Nazis," he replied. "I was luckier than many people. My friend here in Vienna, Herr Doctor Haas, helped me, and I had money in a bank account in Switzerland. I was able to make a home here, to buy a good piano, and to find friends. That's all anyone really needs. Now, enough questions! I must run to the market before it closes, or there will be no dinner for me tonight."

I wanted to ask him about the people he hadn't been able to help, the ones whose faces he used to see in his mind, but I guessed it would be rude. After all, he'd just said I'd asked enough questions.

As I walked home, my thoughts went in circles, like the little horse-drawn buggies that carried tourists around central Vienna's Ring. Herr Hummel had money in a Swiss bank account. Vain Rudolf Beck had begged to take lessons from him. And Beck had thought Herr Hummel had influence at the Horak Conservatory.

I remembered what Frau Vogel had said about my professor's having played in Prague and Paris and Berlin. He must have been a well-known concert pianist. But if that was so, how come he was so poor now? And why hadn't I heard of him? Kurt had known all the good concert pianists in Europe. Some he had met or heard in person, and some he had known through their records and reputations. He had talked for hours about which one had the sweet, golden tone; which the light, quick touch of silver; and which the depth of expression to hold an audience spellbound. But never had he mentioned a Wilhelm Hummel.

I sighed. Herr Hummel's Past was growing more mysterious all the time.

9

Wednesday evening I stood in front of the calendar on the kitchen wall, counting the squares. There were only nine days left to the recital. Nine days ago had been February twenty-first. Why, that had been the day I'd turned in my English essay! It didn't seem like very long ago at all—and now it was only that long again until March eleventh.

At my lesson Friday, Herr Hummel said, "I can tell you've been practicing a lot. You play much more smoothly and confidently, and you have more control. So naturally I will reward you by giving you more difficult music and by being more critical."

"How kind!" I pretended to groan, but I was pleased.

Sunday I stayed at Herr Hummel's until dark. When I got home, Mutti was waiting at the door. Her mouth was a tight line.

"You said you'd be home at four and it's after six!

I've been waiting for you to get here to try on your new dress so I can finish the seams."

I didn't remember saying I'd be home at four. But because I was tired and hungry and eager to try on my new dress, I only mumbled, "I'm sorry. I should have watched the clock."

The dress seams were basted together with pins and loose stitches, so I had to stand very still with my arms outstretched while Mutti walked around me and adjusted the darts and tucks. She wouldn't let me get anywhere near the mirror. It took experience, she always said, to see a dress in the early stages and know how it would look when it was finished. Some of the ladies she sewed for at Herr Rosenwald's would rush over to the mirror with their basted, unhemmed dresses on—and then be in tears at what they saw.

"Are you sure it will be ready by Friday?" I asked her.

Mutti took the pins out of her mouth and stuck them in the little red pincushion. "Yes, I'm sure. You sound like my customers at the shop: 'Will it be finished in time? Are you sure it will be ready for my big day?' And it always is. I've never disappointed anyone."

I didn't say any more, but I still fretted silently.

What if Mutti got sick, or what if she wasn't satisfied with something and wanted to rip out the seams?

. . .

Tuesday was my last lesson before the recital. Herr Hummel paced the floor and listened and instructed while I went through the nasty-looking études. Then I played the Scarlatti sonata.

To my horror, I stumbled only a few measures into it. I began again and stumbled twice.

"You're just nervous," Herr Hummel said comfortingly.

"But I'll be nervous on Friday, too!" I cried. "What if I do the same thing then?"

"Then you will still be a good pianist, and I will still be proud of you, and the world will still keep turning, and the next time you perform you will be less nervous and play better."

"But perhaps I'm not ready to play at the Academy! I've never played in public before and—"

"That's odd." Herr Hummel tilted his head to one side. "I didn't see your mother come in, but I could have sworn I heard her talking just now."

I laughed. I guessed I *had* sounded like Mutti.

I began the Scarlatti again. This time I didn't stumble, but the sonata didn't have the energy it usually did. Neither did the Mendelssohn.

"Perhaps we should stop early tonight," Herr Hummel said. "You sound tired. Take it easy tomorrow, and you'll be fine."

I hoped so. I still felt shaken about faltering in the Scarlatti.

While he was fixing our hot chocolate, I reached up and stroked the angel's gown with one finger. "Wish me luck on Friday," I whispered. Her wise little face under the gold-wire halo seemed to say, "You'll be fine. I'll be with you in your heart." I felt better. Surely no other children in the recital had ever had an angel smile at them.

The next evening, my new dress was ready for me to see myself in. It was perfect! It made me look like a young lady instead of a plumpish schoolgirl. The bodice fit snugly over my new bra and made my waist look smaller than it was. The pleated skirt clung gently to me as I walked, making me look almost willowy.

"It's beautiful, Mutti!" I cried. "I bet no one else in my class has a dress this pretty—not even Elisabeth!"

Mutti looked pleased. "It does do something for you. Let me stitch up the sash and then you can go show Frau Vogel."

Frau Vogel was spending the evening with us, to listen to a speech that Chancellor Schuschnigg was to give from Innsbruck. Her own radio, Eulalie, was broken—probably exhausted, Mutti had told her wryly.

"It's lovely!" she exclaimed when I modeled my dress. "You look very sophisticated—much older than twelve."

Which was exactly what I wanted.

Later, I brought my schoolbooks into the living room so I could sit by the coal stove and do my lessons while Mutti and Frau Vogel listened to the radio. But Schuschnigg's voice—usually so dry and dull—was full of life and energy tonight. I soon laid aside my books and gave my attention to the squat brown radio.

Schuschnigg announced that on the following Sunday, March thirteenth, Austria would have a plebiscite—a special election. The voting would be simple: you would vote Yes if you wanted Austria to remain free, or No if you wanted us to give up our independence and be ruled by Hitler and his Nazis.

"And of course everyone will vote Yes," Frau Vogel said. "Then Hitler will have to leave us alone. He said himself that he would never take over Austria unless we said we wanted him to."

In his native Tyrolean dialect, Schuschnigg was pleading, "Say Yes to Austria! Men, the time has come!"

Our reception faded briefly, but the crackles of

static couldn't hide the jubilation in the thousands of voices that took up Schuschnigg's cry. "*Heil*, Austria! Red-white-red until we're dead! Austria unto death!"

Mutti was sewing so fiercely she ran the needle right into her thumb.

"Ow!" she cried, and stuck her thumb into her mouth.

Frau Vogel chuckled. "Be careful, Anneliese, or Greta will wear a red-white-red jabot at her recital!"

"I'll be so-o-o patriotic!" I giggled.

Mutti didn't laugh. "Blood and death are nothing to laugh about," she said shortly. "I don't like this 'Austria unto death' business. People have forgotten what war is like."

"But you wouldn't want the Nazis to take over Austria, would you?" I asked anxiously. "Herr Hummel says living under them is a nightmare. He says—"

Mutti snorted. "If your Herr Hummel wants to talk about nightmares, let him remember the war. 'Red-white-red until we're dead,' " she mimicked. "Pah! Easy words to say! But wait until it's *your* father, *your* uncles who are going to war. And it's *you* who's starving and ill, standing in line for hours only to be told that there's no more food. Then it's too late to take back those pretty words!"

She was taking short, quick stitches, pulling the thread hard and taut after each one.

"I know, lovey," Frau Vogel said soothingly. Her own husband had been killed fighting on the Russian front, so she knew what war meant as well as anybody.

. . .

The next morning, I didn't hear anything my teachers said. Tomorrow was my recital! New terrors gripped my mind. What if I stumbled the way I had at my last piano lesson and got too flustered to keep playing? What if the piano at the Academy had an uneven touch? What if the streetcar broke down and I was late?

It was a relief to get to music class. Instead of lecturing and asking questions, Frau Gessler (who was very patriotic) played Strauss waltzes on her Victrola. Then she had us sing "The Emperor's Hymn," Austria's national song.

"*Vaterland, wie bist du herrlich!*" we ended gloriously. "*Gott mit dir, mein Österreich!* Fatherland, how splendid you are! God be with you, my Austria!"

Beside me, Elisabeth sniffed. "Hmmph! That's also the tune to *Germany's* national anthem, if old Gessler doesn't know it!"

"It was ours first," I whispered back. "Joseph Haydn wrote it for Austria, so there!"

Frau Gessler looked sharply at us. But before she could scold us for talking, there was a knock at the door. She opened it and took a note from someone outside.

"Ah, how nice!" she exclaimed, reading it. "Class, I need volunteers for a patriotic duty. Who would like to help Austria this afternoon?"

We all looked at one another.

"By doing what, Frau Gessler?" Hedi asked eagerly. "Shooting Herr Hitler?"

"Hedi, really!" Frau Gessler snapped. "Children, stop giggling! Our Chancellor's party, the Fatherland Front, needs volunteers to hand out leaflets to people on the street, telling them to vote for Herr Schuschnigg on Sunday."

Elisabeth waved her hand. "My father would be furious if I did anything to help Schuschnigg. He says—"

"You need not go, Elisabeth," Frau Gessler said quickly. "Who would like to? All right, Greta, Julie, Annemarie, and Trude. Report to the front steps, and the volunteer leaders will tell you what to do. This is a wonderful opportunity for you to help your country. I only wish I could go with you!"

I followed the others out the door. I didn't really think Austria needed my help—after all, nobody with a brain needed to be told to choose our Chancellor

Schuschnigg over that wretched Adolf Hitler. No, I'd volunteered because I knew Herr Hummel would be pleased, and because it would keep me from having to sit through English and history classes, thinking up more disasters that could befall me tomorrow.

Outside, there was enough activity to take my mind off the recital. Austrian marches, polkas, and waltzes poured from people's open windows. Trucks decorated with red-white-red bunting and signs reading SAY YES TO AUSTRIA! drove past, blaring out music and directions to the polls.

My job was easy. I went to the corner of Mariahilfer Strasse and Stumper Gasse and tried to stand straight and tall, like a proud Austrian. When someone came along, I would say, "Hello! Be sure to vote Yes on Sunday!" and hand over a leaflet.

Everyone was pleasant and thanked me with a smile. One woman patted my arm and said, "I already have a leaflet, Fräulein! Save that one for yourself. Someday you will look at it and remember how you helped save Free Austria in March 1938!"

I thanked her and stuck the leaflet in my book bag. I could put it with my recital program and the photos Mutti had promised to take of me in my new dress.

I ran out of leaflets before it was time for school to let out. I thought of running back to school to get more, but it seemed silly. The volunteer leader had said that leaflets were being handed out all over Vienna. They were even fluttering down from the airplanes that had been flying overhead all day.

It also seemed silly to go back for the last part of history class when I was almost home. Nobody would care. Today was like a holiday. As I walked home, Strauss's sweet, glorious *Radetzky* March filled the air. Adults greeted me on the street without even asking why I wasn't in school. Today in Vienna, you could do anything you wanted!

What *I* wanted to do was go home and practice.

I unlocked our door, dropped my books and coat, and had a cookie and a glass of milk. Tomorrow at this time, I thought, I'll be getting ready to come home and put on my new dress. Would I feel prepared? Would I be scared?

I shivered as I sat down at the piano. *Tomorrow, tomorrow!*

After some warm-up exercises, I started my Scarlatti. I stumbled at the same place I had at my lesson. And at another place. And another.

I stopped and stared at the keyboard, stunned. Something was terribly wrong! I was stumbling at places I'd never had trouble before. I sounded stiff and wooden. The notes were just that—notes. They didn't go anywhere, didn't say anything, didn't make music.

I started again. This time I stumbled even sooner. Fingers tripped one another, got in the way.

They were the same fingers I'd always had. What had changed? Only that I knew my recital was tomorrow, and I was scared.

I remembered what Herr Hummel had said: I had to let the music in me chase out the fear. But how could I, when I was playing worse than I ever had?

I took a deep breath, but it came out in a ragged sob. The fear had chased out the music. It was gone. It wouldn't come back in time.

Outside, trucks were driving up and down the street, their loudspeakers playing marches and crying, "Vote Yes for Austria on March thirteenth! Vote Yes for a Free Austria!" I wished they would be quiet.

Suddenly our door buzzer made its familiar ugly sound. I went to the door and hesitated. I didn't want to see anyone.

"Greta?" came a soft voice. "It's me, Lore Siegler. From school. I brought your assignments."

Who? I wrinkled my brow. Oh, yes, Lore Siegler, the little sparrow-girl. I scowled. I had to open the door, since she'd probably heard me playing.

I opened the door and said hello.

"Here are your assignments for English and history," she said in her soft voice. She lowered her eyes shyly as she handed me a sheet of paper.

"Thank you. It was kind of you to bring them."

She stood there for a moment, twisting her hands nervously. Then she looked up and said, "I—I came for a special reason! Frau Schäffer was back today and read some of our essays. Yours was one that she read and—well, I didn't know you were a musician! I am, too. I play viola."

"You do?" I couldn't have been more surprised if Frau Vogel said *she* played the viola!

Lore nodded eagerly. Her eyes glowed with excitement now. They were gray, I noticed, and she had a sprinkling of freckles over her nose. She was pretty when she smiled.

"I took lessons at the Conservatory in Innsbruck. My professor there gave me the name of a friend of his who teaches viola here at the Academy. Do you study there?"

"No, I have a private teacher. But my brother went there and I hope to go there someday. Come on in and we'll talk."

"I can only stay a minute. I have to run some errands for my mother. Did you know that our mothers work together? Mutter has been wanting me to come visit you."

"My mother's been the same, about you," I said, "but that's all right. We can be friends anyway!"

We both laughed, and Lore came into the living room. I told her about the Academy—what a good school it was, who some of the professors were, and where the various lessons were given. "The violists and other string players study in the same building as the piano students," I added. "We can go there after school on Saturday, and I'll show you around!"

"I'd love that." Lore's face was beaming now. "Oh, I'm so glad Frau Schäffer read your essay! The other girls at school are nice, but they're not musicians. They don't really . . ." She shrugged.

"Understand. I know." Even Erika had sometimes gotten impatient with my practicing and talking about music so much.

"Everyone is excited about your recital, though," she went on. "Well, everyone except Elisabeth von Prettin. She just wanted to tell us about the piano she got for her birthday. 'The finest piano in all Vienna!' she said."

"She *would*." Imagine, saying that about the Jacobsons' old piano!

"We're all hoping you'll play your pieces for us

next week sometime. Even Frau Schäffer. She said we can borrow the piano in the music room. But now, tell me about your recital!"

I told her about Herr Hummel's knowing Herr Doctor Haas and my quick preparation of the two pieces. I didn't feel shy or wonder what to say. I even told her how the music had left me.

"Oh, it's always like that the day before a performance!" Lore exclaimed when I told her. "Especially your first one. The day before my first recital, I was so scared I felt like I'd never seen a viola before. But I was fine once I got onstage. You have to relax and trust yourself. Oh! Look at the time! I must go. But I'll see you tomorrow at school, and on Saturday."

"We can have a late lunch in the park afterward!" I called as she started down the stairs.

"Fantastic!"

I went to the living room window and watched her as she walked down Stumper Gasse. She held her head up now, and there was a little bounce in her step.

I was sure we were going to be good friends.

I sat down at the piano again. I closed my eyes.

Trust yourself.

All right, I decided. I will. I'll simply move my fingers and see what happens.

This time I didn't play my recital pieces or anything in particular. All I did was let my right hand move along the keyboard as it wished. I felt relaxed and in control. The music hadn't left me after all.

The tune began to sound like Scarlatti. Feeling dreamy, even a little drowsy, I added my left hand and played through my sonata. It was exactly what I wanted. I played the Mendelssohn. This is how birds feel, I thought. Flying, soaring, sweeping, fluttering, landing.

I kept playing until Mutti got home.

"What a long day! I'm exhausted," she said as she hung her coat in the hallway. "What about you? Did you have a good day?"

"Yes, I did." I smiled to myself. I'd helped save Free Austria, I'd made a friend—and I was finally learning what it meant to believe in myself.

10

My recital day was the kind of warm, springlike day that would make the yellow forsythia buds in our courtyard open early. Only a few little clouds, as light and delicate as a Viennese waltz, drifted across the deep turquoise sky. The gentleness of the day calmed me. How awful if I'd had pelting rain and crashing thunder to rattle my nerves!

I put on my school uniform and curled my hair. I would come home after school long enough to change into my new dress, but I wouldn't have time to do my hair as well.

Last night I had washed my hair and Mutti had trimmed off the split ends. Now each lock was wavy and soft as I unwrapped it from the curling iron. I brushed the front strands to the back of my head and caught them loosely in the gold clasp.

I smelled coffee, heard a chair scrape on the kitchen floor.

"How do you like my hair?" I asked gaily as I walked into the kitchen. Then I stopped, my smile fading. Mutti was still in her bathrobe. She sat at the kitchen table, her forehead resting in one hand.

"What's wrong? Do you have a headache?" I cried.

She shook her head slowly.

"What is it, then? You can still come to my recital, can't you?"

Her words were low, almost a whisper. "Would you mind terribly if I didn't?"

"If you didn't come? But you promised!"

"I know. I thought I could, but I'm just not ready."

I blinked at her, not understanding. *I* was the one who had to be ready!

Mutti shook her head, almost as if she was in a daze. "When I think of having to go there, having to listen to all that piano music, I—I just don't think I can do it. You understand, don't you? I haven't been to the Academy since before Kurt . . ."

Anger roared in my ears. Then, oddly, Schuschnigg's voice: *"The time has come!"*

"Mutti, I miss Kurt, too." My words were like hailstones, hard and frozen. "And I'd give up playing the piano if it would bring him back, but it wouldn't."

"Of course not. I never said—"

"No, you never *said* it, but you *act* like it would!"

Her mouth was open in surprise.

"Mutti, I'm your child, just like Kurt was. But Herr Hummel and Frau Vogel have been my parents more than you've ever been. They believe in me and encourage me! Even if you did come to my recital, you wouldn't be hearing *me*, Greta. You'd be hearing Kurt and seeing Kurt and—and loving Kurt the whole time. There's no place in your heart for me, because it's all filled up with Kurt!"

"Greta!" Her face was shocked and hurt. "You don't really—"

"Yes, I do mean it! And I'm leaving for school now. If you want to come to my recital, come. If you don't, don't. I don't care. I'm tired of caring. I'm going to be a concert pianist, and you can't stop me!"

I ran into the living room, grabbed my book bag, took my coat off the hook in the hallway, and slammed the door as I left.

My heart was pounding. What if Mutti got sick, the way she had when I'd been angry at her for putting the music in the attic? Then she can call Frau Vogel to come stay with her, I told myself sternly. I'd had to say what I'd said.

"Greta, wait!"

Hedi, Käthe, Paula, and Annemarie were running up the walk behind me.

"Tell us about your recital!" Hedi cried.

"Why didn't you let us know you were playing at the Academy?" Käthe asked.

"Oh, look at your hair! It's beautiful!" Paula said.

"What are you wearing?" Annemarie asked. "Not your school uniform, I hope!"

"No, I'm wearing a beautiful blue dress my—my mother made."

"Will you still speak to us when you're famous?" Käthe teased.

"I'll think about it." I laughed. Then, impulsively, I said, "Once the recital's over, I want to celebrate! Maybe you can all come over to my apartment someday next week. I'll invite the new girl, Lore, too. She plays viola, and I'm going to show her around the Academy tomorrow. And I know someone who makes wonderful tortes!"

I thought I saw Hedi and Käthe glance at each other in surprise. Then Hedi said, "That's a terrific idea! I'll be there."

"Me too!" Käthe said.

"Count me in!" Paula grinned.

"I'm free all week," Annemarie said.

"My piano lessons are Tuesdays and Fridays, but the other days will be all right," I said. I could skip practicing for one day. And if Mutti was ill, we could go out to the courtyard or promise to be very quiet.

Funny—it hadn't been hard to invite them at all!

It was an enchanted schoolday. Lore and I ate lunch together. Everyone seemed to have heard about the recital! Girls I barely knew asked me about it or congratulated me. I was still nervous, but I wasn't scared, as I'd been yesterday; I knew now that the music would never leave me.

Elisabeth was very quiet all day. Finally, as we were leaving English, our last class, I felt a tug on my sleeve. In a small voice, Elisabeth asked, "Is it hard to play the piano?"

"Hard?" I laughed airily and tossed my curls exactly the way she always did. "Not for me!"

She looked miserable. "My parents are making me take lessons, but I'm not very good at music. Not—not like you are."

"I've been playing for many years, Elisabeth. I'm sure you'll be fine. You'll only play easy things at first."

For a moment, I thought she was going to smile a real smile at me. But then, like the normal Elisabeth, she said, "Good! I have better things to do than practice the stupid piano!" Then she tossed her curls and flounced away.

When I got home, there was only time to put on my dress, touch up a few curls, and say a quick prayer. Mutti wasn't home, and the gray suit she had planned to wear to the recital was no longer hanging on her door. Perhaps she was coming after all.

"How lovely you look!" Herr Hummel greeted me when I got to his apartment. He looked very fine himself, in a dark blue suit, crisp white shirt, and red-and-blue-striped tie. "Will your mother meet us at the Academy?"

"I think so."

Herr Hummel looked at me quizzically, but I didn't want to talk about Mutti. I'd told myself all day that I didn't care whether she came or not, but I did care. I cared a lot.

We took a streetcar around the southern curve of the Ring, then walked the last few blocks to the Academy. My heart beat faster. I'd come here many times to listen to Kurt. Now I was going to perform. My dream was coming true!

The recital hall where we were playing was small and had no velvet curtains or spotlights. The piano sat on a low stage, with a large arrangement of red and white flowers on one side and the Austrian flag on the other.

Herr Doctor Haas came over to greet us. "Good afternoon, Wilhelm! Fräulein Radky, how good to see you! I was thrilled when Wilhelm told me that you were the student he has been bragging about. I am eager to hear you!"

I said, "*Küss die Hand,*" and gave a little curtsy.

"You'll be playing fifth," Herr Doctor Haas said. "You may go sit with the other performers in the front row. We'll start soon."

"I'll sit in the back and save a seat for your mother," Herr Hummel said. "And don't worry—you'll be fine!"

He squeezed my arm and was gone.

I went up to the front row and sat down. Most of the other pianists were older than I was. Some flexed their hands nervously; others talked and joked. A dark-haired girl in a black dress smiled at me. The boy next to me, tall and thin with glasses and scraggly blond hair, turned to greet me.

"Hello," he said. "What are you playing?"

When I told him, he raised his eyebrows. "Ah, Scarlatti! So few people play Scarlatti well, you know. My professor says most people simply murder the sonatas. I look forward to hearing you!"

"H-how do they murder the sonatas?" I asked. But Herr Doctor Haas was getting up to speak.

The recital started. The first performer was a blond boy named Paul, who played two of Schumann's *Al-*

bum Leaves. Second was a short, chubby girl playing Chopin. Another girl played the Bach prelude I was working on. The girl in the black dress was right before me. She played a Rachmaninoff prelude that Kurt had performed often.

It was almost my turn.

It's all right, I thought. The music will be there, in my hands and in my heart, right where I left it yesterday. But my hands were damp, and my heart was pounding.

I pictured Herr Hummel's little angel, floating in front of the lace curtains. Just picturing her serene little face made me feel stronger, calmer. She seemed to represent all the people who believed in me: Herr Hummel, Frau Vogel, the girls at school—and the growing part of *me* that believed in me.

Then the Rachmaninoff was over, and it was my turn. Herr Doctor Haas introduced me.

My heart pounded as I walked to the piano. Just forget the audience, I told myself, and play to the little angel across town.

The Scarlatti was first. When I touched the keys, a sort of miracle happened: something inside me seemed to take over and play—and it played far better than I could have played myself. The music filled the air with a joy and a clarity it had never had before. I was in perfect control, making some notes as wispy as a bird's breath, others as crisp as winter stars.

Kurt had said that happened sometimes when you performed. A deep inner part of you took over and played while the everyday you listened and marveled at it. Now I understood what he'd meant.

When I finished the sonata, everyone clapped loudly. Some people went "Ahhh!" and I heard someone say "Charming!"

This is fun, I thought. Why had I ever been afraid of the audience? They liked my playing!

So when I played the Mendelssohn, I played not just to the angel but to them, too.

While I played, the everyday me thought everyday thoughts: The piano has a nice touch; someone needs to fasten the curtain that is blowing in the breeze. At the same time, I was hearing the other me caressing the notes, delicately shaping each phrase, timing the pauses perfectly.

When I reached the end, the final chord hung in the air for a few moments, then settled like golden dust over the recital hall. The audience burst into applause. I stood up and curtsied to a blur of smiling faces and clapping hands.

I sat down, weak with happiness and relief. I remembered when Kurt and I had gone to the Hofburg

Palace to see the Imperial Crown. It had been enclosed in a glass case where everyone could see it, but no one could touch it. That was how this day would be for me, I thought. No matter what happened in the rest of my life, today would be safe in its glass case. Nobody could ever mar it or take it away from me.

The long-haired boy was next. He was a powerful, sophisticated pianist, but the piece he played had no melody—just loud crashes and dramatic pauses and wild runs. It was ugly and boring and seemed to go on forever. When people began whispering, I thought it was just because they were as bored as I was. But the whispering didn't stop when the long-haired boy did. If anything, it got even louder while the last three children played. I heard the words "plebiscite" and "Nazis." Politics again! I wanted to tell everyone to be quiet. The last pianist, a boy named Hans, was playing Mozart's Rondo *alla Turca,* one of my favorite pieces, and he was playing so well I wanted to hear him.

Herr Doctor Haas thanked everyone for coming, but he spoke hastily and his eyes were on the door. To my surprise, he ended by saying, "May God bless us and our country in the days to come."

People hurried out of the room, pushing and shoving. They weren't talking about us or our playing but about Hitler and Schuschnigg and radio announcements. Herr Hummel was hurrying toward me, holding out my coat. "You played beautifully! Now hurry, we must get home!"

"But—but what's happening? Where's Mutti?"

"She isn't here, Greta. She couldn't come."

I stared at him, letting people push past me.

She hadn't come.

So that was that.

"It wasn't her fault." Herr Hummel's voice was kind. "Frau Vogel called and had Lothar's secretary bring me a message. Rumors say that Schuschnigg has canceled the plebiscite. The Nazis are rioting all over central Vienna. Your mother couldn't get here. She's all right, though. She got away from the shop and is at Frau Vogel's. We should be happy about that."

Schuschnigg? Rioting? I didn't understand. Surely Mutti could have gotten here if she'd wanted to. It wasn't far from Rosenwald's. All you had to do was cross the Ring and turn—

Herr Doctor Haas came running up. "I'll take you both home in my car. I've heard it isn't safe to be out on the streets."

A car! I'd never ridden in a car before. The idea was exciting. But as Herr Hummel and I waited in the front hall, I thought about how he and Mutti and I were supposed to be celebrating in the garnet and ivory splendor of the Hotel Sacher's dining room. Why did the Nazis have to go and ruin everything?

"I hear that the worst rioting is around Karlsplatz," Herr Doctor Haas said as we got into the front seat. "We'll go in the other direction, toward the park, and made a wide circle south."

Then, as he pulled out onto Lothringerstrasse, I saw the Nazis, thousands of them, filling the streets. I could hear their cries of "*Sieg Heil!*" and "*Heil*, Hitler!"

No wonder Mutti hadn't been able to come to the Academy!

I was thankful to be in Herr Doctor Haas's car with Herr Hummel's arm around me. But why were the Nazis rioting? I looked at the two men, but they were so tense I didn't want to ask them.

It was a long trip to Stumper Gasse, threading our way through back streets. When we finally pulled up in front of Herr Hummel's building, I thanked Herr Doctor Haas and ran ahead of my professor.

To my surprise, Frau Vogel was coming out of Herr Hummel's flat. When she saw me, she gasped with relief. "Greta, lovey! Thank God you're safe! Your mother's here, in Herr Hummel's apartment. I saw her coming from my window. She couldn't climb the stairs, so the superintendent let us in here."

I didn't even ask what she meant, I just ran into Herr Hummel's living room. Mutti was sitting on the sofa, her ankle bandaged and propped up on the coffee table. Her braids had come unpinned, and she had a square white bandage on her forehead. What scared me most was the way her face looked—all trembly and shocked. Her eyes seemed to be still seeing things she'd seen somewhere else.

"Greta!" She reached for me. "You're safe! I tried to come—"

"I know. I saw the Nazis." I put my arms around her. Herr Hummel rushed into the room and sat down on the other side of her.

"Frau Radky, what happened?"

In a dazed voice, she said, "I thought I'd be all right. The Rosenwalds had left to go stay with friends in the country. Everyone else had gone home early. After they left, I saw the Nazis coming, beating up the police, smashing windows. I thought that if they saw me there by myself, if they knew the Rosenwalds were gone, they'd leave the shop alone. I ran up to the workroom and opened a window. I leaned out and cried, 'I'm the only one here! Me, Frau Radky!' "

She was shaking violently.

"Frau Waldmann was there, in the crowd. She yelled—" Mutti's voice broke. "She yelled, 'It's Frau

Radky! She's worse than a Jew because she *works* for Jews!' Frau Waldmann, whose dress I was making! Then I heard someone yell, 'Burn the shop!' More Nazis were coming, screaming that there was a Jew-lover in Rosenwald's shop. They had torches. I ran out the back door. I twisted my ankle, but I didn't dare stop. I ran all the way home. I couldn't go to the Academy, Greta! I tried and I *couldn't*."

"I know, Mutti. It's all right."

Herr Hummel got a blanket to put around Mutti's shoulders. Still she couldn't stop trembling or talking.

"The things I saw! Herr von Prettin was beating an old Jewish man. I think it was Herr Bergen, the jeweler's father. He was on the ground, helpless, and Herr von Prettin kept kicking him. Ilse and Elisabeth were there. They looked ill. Ilse says Elisabeth is terrified of Josef."

I pictured Herr von Prettin's cruel face and suddenly felt sorry for Elisabeth. Ha, I thought, the world *must* be topsy-turvy if I was feeling sorry for Elisabeth von Prettin!

"Try to rest," Herr Hummel told Mutti. "I'll fix us something to eat." He winked at me. "It won't be the Hotel Sacher, but it will have to do."

"The Hotel Sacher?" Mutti asked weakly.

"Yes, we were going there after the recital, remember? To celebrate. And we must still do it some evening, because Greta played beautifully. You would have been proud of her."

"Proud? I am proud. Of course." Mutti looked puzzled, as if she was feeling around in her mind for something. "Greta, I thought about those things you said this morning. You said there wasn't room for you in my heart, but there is!"

"I know, Mutti. We'll talk about it later. Just rest now."

"Perhaps you could come help me fix some food," Herr Hummel suggested quietly to me. "Then your mother may calm down a bit."

I followed him into the kitchen. How odd to think this was where Erika and I had once sat and studied, wolfed down pastries, talked, joked, laughed! Suddenly I envied Erika, safe and secure in America, going sightseeing and watching *Snow White* with Rosemary.

Frau Vogel had made coffee, so I poured us all some and arranged the cups, spoons, and sugar on a tray. Then I spread butter on the thick slices of bread Herr Hummel was cutting.

When we got back to the living room, Frau Vogel had turned the radio louder. It played a waltz as I passed around the tray.

Frau Vogel's plump hands shook as she took her cup off the tray. I began shaking myself. I'd never seen Frau Vogel frightened before.

Herr Hummel was scared, too. He tried not to show it, but I could see it in his eyes.

"We should have known Hitler would never allow Schuschnigg to hold the plebiscite," he said. "He must have known the Nazis didn't have a chance of winning, so he threatened to declare war on Austria if it wasn't canceled."

Suddenly the music stopped. Then we heard Chancellor Schuschnigg's voice, tired and strained. "Austrian men and women! This day has placed us in a tragic and decisive situation."

Herr Hummel had guessed right. The government of Nazi Germany had given our government an ultimatum: either Schuschnigg had to step down and let Hitler appoint a Nazi chancellor to rule us, or Nazi troops would storm in and kill everyone who got in the way. So Schuschnigg was stepping down. Hitler was taking over Austria.

"We are yielding to brute force," Schuschnigg said, "because we do not want bloodshed. So I bid farewell to the Austrian people with a wish from the bottom of my heart: God protect Austria!"

The radio played our national anthem. The record

was old and scratchy, but the courage and sweetness of the tune came through.

I remembered what Elisabeth had whispered in music class. Germany's anthem had the same tune as ours. But how different the words were! "*Deutschland, Deutschland, über Alles!*" theirs went. "Germany, Germany, above all!"

Herr Hummel's words came back to me: "Living under the Nazis is your worst nightmare."

Mutti was crying softly. I patted her arm. Behind her head, the angel's wings glinted gold in the lamplight.

11

Herr Hummel walked Mutti and me home. Mutti had to go slowly and have us support her.

Up on Mariahilfer Strasse, trucks full of ecstatic Nazis were rumbling by. The men screamed out hateful songs, all about bloodshed and the rotting corpses of their enemies. "Die, Jews!" they shrieked. "*Heil*, Hitler!"

On and on the trucks came. All the Nazis in Vienna must have been lying in wait for Schuschnigg's resignation, I thought. Now they were swarming triumphantly over the city, claiming it as their own, just the way ants swarm over a bread crumb you've dropped on the ground, and devour it.

Herr Hummel walked us up to our apartment.

"Stay inside and keep your doors locked," he told us.

"We will," Mutti said quietly.

A terrible thought hit me. What if Herr Hummel was going to leave Vienna in the night without telling us? After all, he'd fled from the Nazis before.

I flung my arms around him. "You be careful, too!"

He laughed in surprise and smoothed my hair. "I'll be all right. Come over tomorrow and we'll have a fine talk about the recital. I know you're bursting to discuss it! But come early. I'm going to Lothar's studio at the Academy around midafternoon. He wants me to listen to a new piano composition he is working on. Not even the Nazis can stop me from hearing it tomorrow!"

I nodded, reassured.

After he left, I helped Mutti to her bedroom. Then I put on my nightgown, shook my hair loose from its gold clip, and hung my new dress back in the bedroom cupboard. I smoothed the lace jabot as I put it in the drawer. How strange that just hours ago I'd been dressing for the recital!

I went into the living room and turned on Radio Vienna to see whether there was any more news. When we'd left Herr Hummel's apartment, the radio had been playing Schubert's *Unfinished* Symphony. Now the sweet strains of Vienna's Schubert had given way to the swelling chords of German marches.

After the music ended, there was the same announcement we'd heard before: Herr Seyss-Inquart, the man Hitler had put in charge of Austria, was saying, "Men and women of Austria! Remember—any resistance to the German army is out of the question!

Unite and help us all to go forward into a happy future!"

Then there was an announcement that the schools in Vienna would be closed until Tuesday. I made a face. Normally I would have been delighted to hear that. But now I was eager to go to school and tell the others about my recital. Besides, Lore and I had planned to go to the Academy tomorrow!

I turned off the radio and went to bed. I put the comforter over my head so I couldn't hear the auto horns blaring and the Nazis yelling. Then I thought about every detail of the recital, hugging the memory close, like an old stuffed toy.

The next morning, I parted the lace curtains in the living room to look out. Nazi flags were draped over balcony railings and hung out of windows on broomsticks and mop handles—anything people could find. Some were real Nazi flags, and some were red-white-red Austrian flags with crude black swastikas sewn or painted on. Some people had even put huge pictures of Adolf Hitler in their windows, with vases of flowers beside them—as though Hitler were a saint!

Mutti came into the kitchen while I was making coffee. She still limped badly, but her eyes looked normal now—as if she was seeing me and the coffeepot, not the Nazis and their torches.

"I was hoping to wake up and find out all this was a bad dream," she said, gesturing toward the window and the Nazi flags outside. She sat down at the table. "Thank you for doing the coffee. I think there's an old cane up in the attic. Maybe you could run up and get it for me."

"All right." I poured us each a cup of coffee, then went up to the attic. The trunks sat where I'd left them, waiting for me to come back and finish sorting the music inside. Perhaps I could do that on Monday, since school would be out.

Kurt's old metal braces clinked against each other as I reached for the cane. I brushed it off with my hand and took it down to Mutti.

"I think I got all the cobwebs off," I told her, propping it against the table beside her chair.

"Thank you." She picked up the cane and turned it over in her hands as if she'd never seen it before. Softly, maybe to herself, she said, "This was Kurt's. He used it when he was getting over his bad spells."

I set the little pitcher of cream on the table and sat down.

Mutti cleared her throat. "Greta, I want to tell you some things."

I nodded. I stirred cream into my coffee, watching the white streaks swirl through the black coffee. They widened until white and black blended into soft, smooth tan.

"You know that Kurt was often in pain, that he couldn't always practice, and that his right arm was getting worse. He could handle things while he was at the Academy. His professors understood what he was going through and allowed him to delay his exams and recitals. But when he began talking with them about his career, they had to be honest with him—and he had to be honest with himself."

Mutti sighed. She looked old and tired. "He knew that as a concert pianist, he would be afraid to go on concert tours. He couldn't even count on doing recording sessions. It wouldn't be long, he said, before the booking agents would start telling one another, 'Don't hire Kurt Radky! He's a good pianist, but he has to cancel too many tours and performances because of illness.' "

"He could have taught," I put in.

Mutti shook her head. "Perhaps a little, privately, at home. But what good music school would hire a young pianist who had recently graduated and had no experience on stage? In short, he didn't know how he was going to make a living. I told him he could always stay here at home, but he wanted to be independent—just like any other young man.

"When Kurt was in the hospital the last time, he told me not to be sad if he died. He said there was no future for him in music. He said that to make a living, he would have to give up music—and that he'd rather die."

Kurt had been going to give up music? I must have heard wrong.

Mutti raised her eyes to mine. "That's why it's been so hard for me to hear you play the piano. You seem to do it so easily! For Kurt it was so hard—and he knew he'd lose the battle."

"I understand," I said quietly. "But what do you want me to do? Give up music because Kurt had to? I *can't*! And he wouldn't have wanted me to."

"No, of course not." Mutti took a handkerchief out of her bathrobe pocket and blew her nose. "That's the other part of what I wanted to tell you. Yesterday, after you left for school, I realized that you had a handicap, too: you had no parent to help and encourage you. And like Kurt, you fought your handicap. You arranged for your own lessons, and practiced whenever I was out, and were even willing to play at your first recital all alone!"

"I wasn't alone," I put in. "Herr Hummel was there."

"Yes, but I knew I should be there, too. You were

right when you said that he and Frau Vogel were more like parents than I." Mutti wiped her eyes with the handkerchief.

"Yesterday," she continued, "I felt very proud of you for your commitment to music, for not giving up. I realized what a special person you are, and I also realized that if I didn't change quickly, I'd lose you every bit as much as Kurt. I—I don't want that to happen."

She reached out and put her hand over mine.

I smiled at her and said quietly, "I don't want it to happen either, Mutti."

The telephone rang, making us both jump. I ran to answer it.

It was Frau Rothmann, the nearsighted little assistant at the dress shop. Mutti hobbled into the living room with her cane and took the telephone quickly.

"Have you heard anything?" she asked. Then, "Ahhh, thank God! Yes, it's dreadful, but at least they're alive."

After hanging up, she told me what had happened. The Rosenwalds had given up their plan to return to Vienna, and had let their friends take them over the border to Hungary.

"They're safe, but they have nothing," Mutti said.

"They couldn't get back here to get any money or valuables, and Jews aren't allowed to leave Austria with anything of value anyway. Can you imagine? They spent their lives building up that shop, and now they have nothing but the two suitcases they left Vienna with!"

I never thanked them for my blue crepe, I thought, hot with shame. I knew it wasn't important, but just the same I wished terribly that I had.

"The shop wasn't burned after all," Mutti went on. "It's to be given to a good Nazi as a prize." Suddenly her fist banged the wall so hard the telephone jumped. "I won't work for those hoodlums! I'm not going back there, not after last night. I'm sure no one else will, either."

I gasped. "But where will you work?"

Mutti hesitated, but when she spoke her voice was firm. "I shall take in customers myself, here at home. People have suggested it to me over the years. A lot of women like my designs and my sewing, and I think I can be successful."

"That's a wonderful idea!" I cried.

I could practically see Mutti's mind racing. "I could turn Kurt's old bedroom into a workroom. Do you think he'd mind?"

"I'm sure he wouldn't," I said. "He'd be proud of

you. But, Mutti, I'll still have to practice, you know."

"I know that." She smiled. "Perhaps some music will do me good. As a matter of fact, why don't you play your recital pieces for me this evening? You can wear your new dress, just the way you did yesterday! We can have coffee and torte afterward."

I laughed. "I'll give you a command performance, as if you were an empress!"

Frau Vogel came over at lunchtime. She'd been shopping and brought us bread and milk, as well as homemade soup and half of a juicy plum cake she'd made. We could have that after my command performance, I thought, putting it under the glass torte cover. The soup and fresh bread we would have now, for lunch.

"Herr Müller came up and fixed Eulalie." Frau Vogel sighed. "But the poor dear isn't the same. She used to play such *nice* music. Now she plays those great thumping marches that Herr Hitler likes so well. And the news isn't real news anymore, it's people shrieking about the greatness of Germany!"

"Are the Nazis still rioting?" I asked her, setting three soup bowls on the table.

"No, today they are busy rounding up all the Jewish men, even the old and ill ones. They make the men scrub the anti-Nazi slogans from the sidewalks and walls, using their own toothbrushes and pails of acid cleaner that burn their hands. And people taunt and kick them while they work—the same people who yesterday were kind and sensible! I tell you, Vienna is going crazy."

I thought of old Herr Ornstein, whose gnarled, arthritic hands had once summoned forth beautiful cello music. Were those hands having to clean sidewalks now?

I stopped ladling soup into my bowl. I wasn't as hungry as I had been.

Frau Vogel continued. "Thousands of Jews and anti-Nazis were arrested in the night. I heard about it in the market. You've heard of the Nazis' special forces, the *Schutzstaffel*—the SS? They went around to people's houses during the night. They woke people up and hauled them away to prison camps, still in their pajamas."

I shivered. How could things like that happen?

Suddenly I wanted terribly to go to Herr Hummel's. I wanted to sit under the angel and talk and drink hot chocolate and forget about the Nazis.

The telephone rang again. This time it was for me. Lore.

"Greta, how was your recital?"

"Wonderful!"

"I knew it would be! I can't wait to hear all about it, but my mother is waiting for the telephone. She won't let me go out today because of what happened to Käthe Neff. Did you hear?"

"No." My heart pounded.

"She was beaten up by the Nazis last night on her way home from Hedi's. A neighbor told us. The Nazis thought she was Jewish because of her dark hair and eyes."

"But she's Catholic!" I cried.

"She said she told them that, but they either didn't believe her or didn't care. She's all bruised and has a black eye."

Sweet, harmless Käthe Neff! After Lore hung up, I stared at the phone. Why, Käthe was so Catholic she'd even thought of becoming a *nun*, and she'd still been beaten—just because she had dark hair and eyes!

"Who was it, Greta?" Mutti called.

"It was for me," I said, going back into the kitchen. "Someone from school."

I decided quickly that I wouldn't tell Mutti and Frau Vogel about Käthe. If I did, Mutti would never let me go to Herr Hummel's. As it was, she sighed when I asked her.

"Oh, Greta, I don't want you going out alone, not when all the Nazis in Vienna will be out celebrating. Why, I heard on the radio that Adolf Hitler himself may be here tonight! It's no time for you to be out by yourself. You can go in the morning."

"Please!" I begged. I wanted so badly to see Herr Hummel!

"She can walk home with me when I go," Frau Vogel said. "I'll look out for her."

"All right," Mutti told me reluctantly. "You can go with Frau Vogel, and have Herr Hummel walk you home afterward."

"I will," I promised.

But Mutti and Frau Vogel started talking about Mutti's plans to open her own dressmaking business. They discussed ideas and wrote up plans on my school tablet, then crossed them out and discussed new ideas. I paced the floor in the living room. Herr Hummel had said to come early because he was going to the Academy around midafternoon.

I wrote a note to Erika. I knew she would read about Vienna in the newspapers and worry about us.

Finally Frau Vogel said, "Greta, I'm going now!"

"Be careful." Mutti kissed me on the cheek. "I'm going to lie down, but wake me up when you get home. Remember, you're going to give me a command performance tonight!"

I hugged her and whispered, "I love you, Mutti."

"I love you, too," she whispered, and kissed me again, on top of the ear this time.

Outside, the air was filled with sounds from Mariahilfer Strasse. Unlike last night's sounds, these weren't of destruction and hatred but of construction and joy. Hammers pounded, people laughed, and huge banners unfurled with a *whoosh*. Everyone was preparing for the visit of our new leader, our Führer, Adolf Hitler.

"Greta," Frau Vogel whispered urgently, "if anyone says, '*Heil*, Hitler' to you, you must say '*Heil*, Hitler' in return. That's how we have to greet people now. God will know that your heart isn't meaning what your mouth is saying."

I nodded, thinking of what had happened to Käthe. All I wanted was to be invisible to the Nazis. If they spoke to me, I'd just mumble, "*Heil*, Hitler," and hope they'd go on their way.

Frau Vogel went upstairs to her flat. I knocked and knocked on Herr Hummel's door, but there was no answer.

He'd already gone! I could have wept. Now I'd have to wait until tomorrow.

I gave a huge sigh and felt around in my pockets for the key he'd given me. At least I could go inside. Herr Hummel had promised to loan me another volume of *Songs Without Words*. I wanted to work on a new Mendelssohn for my next lesson.

"Good afternoon," I said softly to the angel. I didn't have to say "*Heil*, Hitler" to *her*!

I took the Mendelssohn, Opus 102, from the cupboard shelf. I knew Herr Hummel wouldn't mind if I borrowed it.

I looked at the Bösendorfer grand. It would feel good to play again. Mutti was taking a nap, and I didn't want to wake her. So why didn't I stay here and play for a while? Maybe Herr Hummel would come home early.

I sat down at the piano, opened the book, and began to play the first piece. The tune seemed sad, bewildered, tense. I knew that whenever I played it, I would think of today—of sitting in Herr Hummel's empty apartment, hearing the hateful cries of the Nazis outside and longing to see my professor.

I played the first piece through twice. The second also looked sad, so I skipped to the third one. It was a spirited little piece that sounded as if someone had spilled open a cage of mice. I laughed as I heard my little mice notes scampering and imagined someone trying to catch them.

I finished, and started again. This time I could make the mice run even faster and make their tiny feet even lighter. Now nobody could catch—

A knock on the door startled me. It was dark in the

apartment now, outside the circle of light from the lamp. On my way to the door, I pressed the light switches in the living room and hallway.

The knocking grew louder.

"I'm coming!" I grumbled. Neither Frau Vogel nor Herr Hummel would bang on the door that way. Maybe it was a neighbor who was trying to rest after last night's revels and was annoyed by my playing.

Angrily I unbolted the door and pulled it open.

"Good evening, Fräulein," said a Viennese policeman. "We wish to speak to your professor."

With him were another policeman and two men in military uniforms. On their collars, the jagged silver letters "SS" blazed like twin lightning bolts.

12

The cool voice continued. "We are looking for a Herr Wilhelm Hummel. Is this his address, Fräulein?"

Slowly I nodded.

The men swept inside. The hallway was filled with starched uniforms, shiny boots, pistols, swastikas, lightning bolts.

"Now, Fräulein, you will go and get Herr Hummel, please," the blond SS officer said. He had a long nose and a mustache that was chopped off like Hitler's. "Tell him his friend Rudolf Beck sent us here."

"Rudolf Beck!" I gasped.

The officer's thin lips drew back in a smile. "Herr Beck is a good Nazi. He spent many days tracing your Herr Hummel to this apartment because he knew that we would want to have a little talk with your professor. Now you will get Herr Hummel, please."

"Herr H-hummel isn't here." I hardly recognized the wobbly, faint voice as mine.

"Where is he?"

"He's . . . he's . . ." If only someone were there to help me—Mutti or Frau Vogel or another adult! They'd know what to say.

Suddenly the light caught something shiny, high up in the living room. The angel!

I felt calmer now, more able to think. Where would Herr Hummel be likely to go if he were escaping?

"He's gone to—to Prague," I said. I cleared my throat and continued in a stronger voice. "He left last night. He has friends there, and he—he likes the food."

The other SS officer, with slicked-back dark hair and a heavy oval face, said, "Who are you, and why are you here if your Herr Hummel has gone to Prague?"

I thought quickly. It would be easier if I told the truth.

"I'm Anna Margareta Radky, a pupil of Herr Hummel's. He lets me borrow his piano. My mother is often ill, and—"

"But the superintendent said he has let no one in this evening."

"Herr Hummel gave me an extra key."

"Show it to us!"

I reached for my coat, which was hanging on a hook. My trembling hand dug into the pockets. The key was in the left one. When I pulled it out, the blond SS officer grabbed it and tried it in the door. After he had made sure it worked, he dropped it into his own pocket.

"How do you know your professor has gone to Prague?" he asked.

I cleared my throat. "He told me last night. He stopped by our apartment on the way to the train station. I was listening to the radio, to the music and to Seyss-Inquart. My mother was asleep. Herr Hummel had a suitcase. He said he was going to visit friends in Prague. He said he'd be back next week."

I didn't know why I'd put that last part in, but it made the men laugh.

"Your teacher won't be back, Fräulein!" the blond one said. "Not unless he's a total fool."

One of the policemen said slowly, "There was a train to Brno and Prague that left at eleven-fifteen. This man you're looking for is not a Jew, and he would have had a German passport. He could have slipped across the border as easily as anything."

The men were silent. They're going to leave now, I thought.

Then the other policeman stepped forward. He gave an ugly laugh and said, "Let's search the flat. Who knows? Maybe we'll find a pianist hiding in a cupboard! And if not, perhaps we'll find other things of value. After all, if this man has left Austria, all his belongings are property of the Nazis now."

The blond SS officer nodded. "We'll each take a room. And you, Fräulein, you'll play for us while we search. That will keep you out of trouble!"

"Pl-play?"

"Yes, the piano! After all, you're a student of the great Karl von Engelhart, aren't you?"

"Why, of course not, I'm—" I stopped and stared at him.

"What's the matter?" He was laughing. "Why, you really didn't know, did you? You thought his name actually was Wilhelm Hummel! I suppose he also didn't tell you why he left Germany. It's too bad he's gone, Fräulein, or he could tell you all about how he uses his fortune to help Jewish artists leave Germany. And about how he refused to play for a radio broadcast that Herr Goebbels, our Minister of Propaganda and Enlightenment, was preparing."

Images swirled through my head: Herr Hummel not wanting to talk about his life; Herr Doctor Haas agreeing to let me play in his recital without my even auditioning, just because I was Herr Hummel's student; and Rudolf Beck, so furious at being rejected by Herr Hummel that he'd sent the SS here.

So Herr Hummel was Karl von Engelhart. *That* was his Past! The thought made me so dizzy I had to put a hand on the wall to steady myself. Then, just as suddenly, it made perfect sense, and I felt as if I'd known it forever. All that mattered now was getting rid of the SS and the police.

"Play, Fräulein! Play that piece you were playing when we knocked. It sounded like a jolly tune!"

I sat down at the piano and began the mice piece.

The blond SS officer was searching the living room. He didn't merely search, though. He kicked over the furniture and threw books onto the floor. He ripped apart the sofa cushions with a knife. He didn't have to do that, I thought. Not to those cozy old sofa cushions where Erika and I had played, and where Herr Hummel and I had sat to have our hot chocolate after my lessons.

Then he folded down the door of the little writing desk. A picture flashed through my mind: Schillings. A passport.

Herr Hummel's passport was in the secret compartment! If the SS man found it, he'd know I was lying—that Herr Hummel was still in Austria. He'd beat me; he'd make me tell where Herr Hummel really was.

I stumbled in the Mendelssohn and saw the SS man turn sharply to look at me. Sweat burst out on my brow. I bowed my head over the keyboard and kept playing. Please, God, don't let him find the little brass button, I prayed. Please, God, make me brave.

The officer rifled through some papers, threw them to the floor, and slammed the drop-front door shut. *Bang*! I jumped. He had kicked the desk over on its side. He was mad because he hadn't found anything.

The four men gathered in the wrecked living room.

"I found nothing," the dark SS officer growled.

"We found only a little cash," one of the policemen said.

I finished the mice piece and began the first one in the book, the sad, tense one. God, don't let them ask me any more questions, I prayed, and, oh, God, don't let Herr Hummel come home early.

The blond officer was standing beside me, looking over my shoulder at the music. Suddenly he reached out and snatched it.

I cried out.

He looked at me and smiled, as if he thought it was funny that he was scaring me. Then slowly, deliberately, he tore the music into pieces. He watched my face the whole time. When he was done, he tossed the pieces into the air so that they scattered over my lap, the piano keys, the floor.

"Mendelssohn," he grunted. "A Jew. You are forbidden to play music written by Jews, Fräulein. You won't forget again."

I shook my head, unable to speak. He smiled down his nose at me. Then he turned to the others and motioned toward the door.

"Von Engelhart is gone. He's sitting in Prague, stuffing himself with sausages. Now we must hurry if we are going to join the torchlight procession for our Führer. Come!"

They slammed the door and were gone.

I sat there on the piano bench, shaking all over.

"I'm safe," I told myself, hardly believing it. "It's over. I can go home now. Frau Vogel will walk me home."

But what if Herr Hummel walked out of the Academy straight into the hands of the SS?

Somebody had to warn him. *I* had to warn him.

I jumped up from the piano bench, then made myself sit back down and think. Herr Hummel might have to leave Austria now, tonight, without even coming back here. What would he need? Clothes, I thought, and money, and a passport.

I couldn't help with the clothes. I wouldn't know what to pack, and I could hardly carry a suitcase full of men's clothes through Vienna anyway.

But I could take him his passport, and I'd give him the few Schillings I'd left for my lessons.

I closed the shutters over the windows, then stood the desk upright and pulled out the little drawer. What if the passport was gone? My finger trembled as it pushed the button.

The passport was still there, with my Schillings in it. I took it out and reached for the envelope, to see whether it held anything else Herr Hummel might need. Inside it were bankbooks and so much German and Austrian money that I gasped.

I kept out enough of my Schillings to pay my streetcar fare, since I hadn't brought any money. The rest I put into the envelope. It was a tiny amount compared to what was already in there, but I wanted Herr Hummel to have it. I put the passport into the envelope with the money, then sealed the flap so nothing would fall out.

I got my coat. There was a little hole in the right pocket I'd kept forgetting to tell Mutti about. Now I was glad it was there. I ripped it wider and wider, until I could drop the envelope down into my coat lining. Then I closed both the desk and the cover of the piano for the last time.

Before leaving, I did one more thing. I couldn't take the piano or the desk, but I wouldn't let the Nazis have the angel. Quickly I pulled on the threads that held her. They snapped, and she was safe in my hand. I put her in the good left pocket of my coat. If she made a bulge, people would think it was from mittens.

As I folded the little angel's wings to put her in my pocket, something occurred to me. "My father gave her to my mother the first Christmas they were married," Herr Hummel had said.

A little *Engel*, an angel, for the new Frau von Engelhart!

I put on my coat and left without looking back.

Stumper Gasse had never seemed so long. All those dancing swastikas seemed to know what I was doing, to whisper my secret. And the huge pictures of Hitler! Nearly every window showed the profile of his face, fervent and dedicated, gleaming white in the dusk. I expected him to turn at any moment, to bark out, "We hang people who help our enemies escape, Fräulein!"

My heart pounded as I waited for a streetcar. Streetcars and subways had quit operating last night during the celebrations. What if they hadn't started running again? It was nearly an hour's walk to the Academy. Surely Herr Hummel would be gone by then.

Finally a red-and-white streetcar slid to the curb. I got on and gave the conductor my fare.

"*Heil*, Hitler!" he said as he handed me my change.

I swallowed. If I was going to get Herr Hummel's passport and money to him safely, I would have to pretend to be a Nazi.

"*Heil*, Hitler!" I said, so enthusiastically that the conductor chuckled.

Few people were on the streetcar. I sat down halfway back and looked out the window as though I had nothing on my mind.

All the streets were decked out with Nazi banners and flags. Posters were everywhere: ADOLF HITLER BRINGS WORK AND BREAD! ONE PEOPLE, ONE REICH, ONE LEADER! Some of the posters had ugly caricatures of dark, hook-nosed Jews. JEWISH BLOOD SPURTS FROM NAZI KNIVES! they said. The Nazis had hung those posters on the shops with the shattered windows—the ones belonging to Jews.

Downtown Vienna was full of Nazis. When we got to the Opera House, the streetcar stopped. *Klang, klang!* went the bell. The driver swore. Outside, the crowd was filling the Ring, blocking our path. "*Sieg Heil! Sieg Heil!*" people screamed, waving their torches as they gave the triumphant Nazi cry.

We inched forward, then stopped. The clock by the Opera House said six-thirty. How long would Herr Hummel stay at the Academy? Where should I look if he wasn't there? What if the SS found him before I did?

No, I couldn't let myself think of that.

I got off the streetcar and ran down the street. As I pushed my way through the people, I could feel the envelope shift in my coat lining. Farther and farther back it went, until it bumped me behind the knees. I was glad I could feel it. That way I knew it was still safe.

"Why, Greta Radky!" came a surprised voice.

I looked around and my heart seemed to stop. Frau von Prettin had her hand on my sleeve. With her were Herr von Prettin and Elisabeth.

"You came to the torchlight celebration alone, Fräulein Radky?" Herr von Prettin asked, looking surprised.

"Yes," I replied, thinking quickly. "Mutti has hurt her ankle and can't walk. But she didn't want me to miss the celebration! She said I would remember it all my life."

"We've had word that Herr Hitler won't be here until tomorrow or Monday," Frau von Prettin put in. "But the celebration will continue!"

"You can march with us, Greta," Elisabeth said happily. "Can't she, Vater?"

"Of course!" Herr von Prettin said.

"Thank you." I tried to smile. "But I'm afraid I can't march with you. I—I have to meet someone."

"We'll go with you to find your friend," Frau von

Prettin said. "Your mother wouldn't want you to be alone in this crowd."

"Thank you, but I—I—uh—" I floundered. Then I had an inspiration. "You see, it's a *boy*! I'm meeting a *boy*!"

"Greta!" Elisabeth clapped her hands gleefully. "Let me guess. You're meeting Hedi Witt's brother Konrad!"

"Uh—well—it's a secret, Elisabeth. But I have to go now!"

The von Prettins' laughter followed me as I ran.

By the time I got to the Academy, I was panting for breath. The bells of St. Stephan's Cathedral and all the other Viennese churches had begun to ring, celebrating the marriage of Germany and Austria.

I swung open the door of the Academy. From behind studio doors came the sounds of pianos, violins, cellos. No matter who governed Austria, musicians still had to practice.

I ran up the stairs and down the hall toward Herr Doctor Haas's studio. Could it have been only yesterday that I'd been here, wearing my new dress and thinking that nothing in life mattered except my recital?

As I ran down the hall, I began to hear a piano playing a Liszt rhapsody. The notes fell like a waterfall of clear, pure, crystal drops through which the sun shone and made rainbows. It was music such as Karl von Engelhart would make.

I threw open the door to Herr Doctor Haas's studio.

"Greta?"

Then my face was pressing into Herr Hummel's old blue sweater and his arms were around me.

"They came for you!" I whispered. I closed the door and told him what had happened, how Rudolf Beck had sent the SS. Then I twisted around to pull the envelope out of my coat lining. "You'll need this. It's your passport and money."

Herr Hummel stood there, looking all pale and trembly. Maybe he's too old for a shock like this, I thought. So instead of burying my face in his sweater again, as I wanted to, I took his arm and said, "Come sit down. You'll be fine, really!" and helped him to the piano bench.

"The SS men were very stupid," I chattered. "They looked in the desk, but they didn't see the button for the hidden compartment. I knew about it because the desk once belonged to the Brauners. Erika and I—"

"Did they hurt you?"

"Who, the SS? Why, no! But they—" I stopped. I'd been going to say, "They tore up your flat." Then I thought, no, I wanted him to remember it the way it had been. "But they told me who you are. Why didn't you tell me?"

He thought a moment and, sounding stronger now, said, "Would you have asked to take piano lessons from Karl von Engelhart?"

Slowly I shook my head. "I—I suppose not."

"I know you wouldn't have. Why, you were nervous enough, asking for lessons from plain Wilhelm Hummel!" he said, smiling a little. "I had to have a new name so I could escape from Germany. I was in trouble with the Nazis for helping Jews escape, among other crimes. Wilhelm is my middle name, and Hummel was my mother's maiden name. I had friends who made a passport for me in that name." He shrugged. "And on the train to Vienna, I found I *liked* being Wilhelm Hummel. I wanted to live quietly, without fans pestering me and Nazis trying to trick me into returning to Germany. Do you understand?"

I nodded. "Frau Vogel thought you'd had an unhappy love affair." I tried to giggle, but it came out like a hiccup.

He smiled. "I hope she won't be disappointed." Then he put his big hands on my small ones and said solemnly, "Greta, you risked your life for me, and I'll never forget it."

I suddenly felt shy. "I brought you the angel. See?"

I held her out to him, but he pushed my hand back.

"She'll be safer with you. You must put her over your piano and think of me when you practice."

We both jumped as the door opened. It was Herr Doctor Haas. He listened calmly, without expression, while I told him what had happened.

"I'll take you over the Czech border," he said quietly to Herr Hummel. "It will be safer than the train."

Herr Hummel started to protest, but Herr Doctor Haas held up a hand. "I insist! We should leave immediately. The Nazis are busy celebrating, and the border guards may not be well organized yet. Can you be ready in ten minutes? I'll bring my car around."

Herr Hummel nodded. The dazed look was on his face again.

Herr Doctor Haas said, "Good. We'll stop by my apartment and pick up a few things you'll need." He nodded to us and left.

From outside, the bells had started ringing again. The deep-toned bell of St. Stephan's sounded mournful to me now. I had to press my lips together to keep the tears back.

"Where will you go?" I asked him. "Prague?"

"Yes. Your instincts were good when you told the SS I had gone there. It's easy to get to, and I have friends there."

Will I ever see you again? I wanted to ask. But I was scared of what the answer would be.

We sat silently for a few moments. Finally Herr Hummel drew a handkerchief across his eyes. "Rudolf Beck was certainly right when he said he'd get even with me someday."

He sighed and stood up. "Now we must find someone who will walk you and the angel home. I think Johann Stolz, one of Lothar's students, will do it. He's a good boy. Come along, we'll ask him."

I followed Herr Hummel down the hall. Johann Stolz was in a practice room, pounding out a difficult-sounding étude. He was the homeliest boy I'd ever seen: big and serious, with a round face, pug nose, and very thick glasses over his pale eyes. He looked like a huge, strange bug. I had an impulse to giggle. If the von Prettins saw us, they'd think this was the boy I'd come to meet! I wished there were time to explain the joke to Herr Hummel, but already Johann was gathering up his music and Herr Hummel was giving me a last quick hug.

"Take care of yourself, Greta," he said softly. "I thank you again for saving my life. And don't worry, I'll get out safely!"

I nodded and tried to smile.

"I mustn't keep Lothar waiting." Herr Hummel kissed my forehead and was gone.

Suddenly my mind was filled with things I wanted to tell him: that Mutti and I had talked, that I was making a new friend, that I'd never forget him as long as I lived. I thought of opening a window and calling to him. But, no, I could hardly cry "Herr Hummel!" when the streets below were full of SS men and loyal Nazis.

I followed Johann silently down the stairs and out onto Lothringerstrasse. Snow clouds were gathering in the night sky. The crowds of people weren't cold, though; they were warm with the heat of excitement: *"Sieg Heil! Sieg Heil!"*

I was glad when Johann began talking, asking me whether I played the piano, whether I was Kurt Radky's sister, whether I was going to attend the Academy someday. Answering kept me from thinking. And it was important not to think, because if I did I would cry, and people might stop and ask me why I was crying on this night of our new Führer's glorious victory.

The tears would have to wait.

March 15, 1939

I gave my command performance for Mutti the next evening, when I was less shaken. It was a bittersweet occasion. Bitter because Herr Hummel was gone, the Rosenwalds were gone, and out in the streets the Nazis cried their hateful cries and sang their hateful songs. Sweet because Mutti sat and listened to me play, as she had once listened to Kurt, and because Herr Doctor Haas had stopped by that day to tell me that Herr Hummel was safe in Prague. I played, not my recital music, but Bach and Schumann. I didn't have the heart to play my recital pieces with Herr Hummel gone. And I couldn't play my new Mendelssohn songs: the book was in tiny pieces all over the Nazis' new Bösendorfer piano.

Today, a year and two days later, the Nazis are again rejoicing. Hitler's troops have invaded Czechoslovakia, and they have just raised the swastika over Prague. And once again in a bittersweet way, I am rejoicing—because once again Herr Hummel has escaped them.

We have written each other over the past year, careful letters that we knew might fall into unfriendly hands. Herr Hummel has taken a teaching position at the Curtis Institute of Music in Philadelphia, America. He will sail from Le Havre, France, next week. Yesterday I received a postcard of the Eiffel Tower that he sent me from Paris. His message was brief: "Until then." But it told me all I needed to know: that he was out of Prague and that he wouldn't forget that someday I am to join him at the Curtis Institute, where he will be my teacher again. (I will see Erika then, too; the maps show that New York is very close to Philadelphia!)

Mutti and Frau Vogel and I are also leaving Vienna. The women who flocked to Mutti at Rosenwald's won't come to her now, because she once worked for Jews. We're going to Bern, Switzerland, where she has cousins. They have found her a job as head dressmaker, and we will all three live in a furnished flat over the shop. Frau Vogel hopes to buy a small bakery and fulfill her own secret dream.

Mutti is sad because Kurt's grave is here in Vienna, but she is a stronger person than she used to be. She seldom has headaches now; she says she is too busy trying to make ends meet and planning for our move.

I feel sad about leaving Vienna, too. And I will miss the other girls—especially Lore, who is now my close friend. But her family also hopes to move to Switzerland, to Lore's aunt's home in Basel. Käthe's family plans to move to London; Hedi's, to Ireland. Annemarie's and Paula's families have already left for France. So even if we stayed, my friends would be gone. Besides, the Nazis have turned Vienna into a city of hatred and fear. It no longer seems like my home.

People whisper that war will come. They say that Hitler can't continue marching over Europe, that surely somebody will try to stop him. When that happens, we will be happy to be safe behind that wall of mountains.

We can afford to take only a few trunks with us to Switzerland. But Mutti has promised that as soon as we get settled, we will buy a new piano. She knows that I will have to practice hard if I am going to be good enough to go to the Curtis Institute in America. I don't know how fine a piano it will be, because we will not have very much room or very much money. But I do know one thing: over that piano will fly a tiny, blue-gowned angel who loves piano music.